"Please," Kelloway said to the astronauts, "you have to do this thing. You *have* to!"

"What the hell does that mean?" demanded Brubaker. "What do you mean we have to?"

"You have to," said Kelloway in a low voice.

"What if we don't?"

"Your families," murmured the NASA Director, head down.

"What about our families?"

Kelloway took in a hesitant breath. "They're flying back. There's a device . . . on the plane with them," he said. "There are these people, powerful people. If I don't give them the all-clear signal by a certain time . . . , they'll explode the device."

CAPRICORN ONE

RON GOULART

FAWCETT GOLD MEDAL • NEW YORK

CAPRICORN ONE

© 1978 Peter Hyams Productions, Inc.

Based on a screenplay by Peter Hyams and published by Fawcett Gold Medal Books, a unit of CBS Publications, the Consumer Publishing Division of CBS Inc.

ISBN 0-449-14024-5

Printed in the United States of America

10 9 8 7 6 5 4 3 2

CHAPTER 1

THE SUN, an intense orange ball, began to rise over the Atlantic. A gentle breeze brushed at the blue water.

"Good morning, ladies and gentlemen. This is Paul Cunningham, Capricorn Control. The time is 3 minutes after 6, Eastern Standard Time. We are coming up on T-minus 3 hours, 31 minutes, 25 seconds . . ."

Something was looming in the distance. A tiny white needle on the morning horizon.

"At the present time all systems are go, and all lights are green. At T-minus 8 hours, 5 minutes,

Launch Complex 39 was cleared and we began to load the liquid propellent into the launch vehicle. The loading was completed at T-minus 3 hours, 38 minutes . . ."

The voice echoed slightly in the dim motel room. On the edge of the wide rumpled bed the nearly naked redhaired girl sat, leaning slightly forward, watching the television.

The white needle grew larger and larger on the color screen. It grew until it was recognizable as a towering Saturn MB V rocket. Rising as high as a 35-story building, weighing over six million pounds, gleaming white in the new day.

"The crew was awakened at T-minus 4 hours, 30 minutes, without any major complaints. At T-minus 4 hours, 5 minutes they were taken to the medical complex. They were examined by Dr. Burroughs, who pronounced them fit. The examination lasted until T-minus 3 hours, 45 minutes."

The girl uncrossed and recrossed her long tan legs.

The lean, tangle-haired man who was still asleep between the twisted sheets rolled over on his back. He began making a nasal moaning sound.

"Hush," said the girl, looking at the TV screen. "This is a historical moment. I don't want to miss anything."

There were four men in the prefabricated room. Three of them, each clad in thermal long john, were seated around a folding table, eating breakfast with varying degrees of interest and enthusiasm. The fourth man, wearing a wrinkled blue suit, was leaning against the metal wall and rubbing his thumb across his plump chin.

"Weather is good," said the pudgy Burroughs. "Scattered clouds until noon, that's about all."

"You already told us," said Air Force Colonel Charles Brubaker. "Twice."

"Oh, sorry," said the NASA medic.

Navy Commander John Walker tapped black fingers on a half-eaten slice of toast. "This toast tastes like that stuff you stick memos on," he said. "Corkboard."

"It's left over from a previous mission," suggested Lieutenant Colonel Peter Willis. "NASA's recycling it to save money."

"Just wait," said Burroughs. "In a few days you'll miss food like this."

"Down-home Earth cooking," said Walker, deciding to take a couple more bites of the toast. "Corkboard."

"Tasted fine to me when I breakfasted." Dr. Burroughs stuffed his pudgy hands into the wrinkled pockets of his trousers.

"I hope nobody ever finds out about this," said Brubaker, a tall, slightly thickset man in his early forties. "Here it is the morning of man's first venture to another planet, and all we can talk about is toast."

"I hope they don't find out that on the morning of man's first venture to another planet," put in Walker, "they gave us such crappy food."

"The toast really tasted fine to me," reiterated Burroughs. "And I don't usually like whole wheat bread."

Willis, thinner and several years younger than the others, pushed back from the table and slapped both knees. "What would you like to talk about on such a momentous occasion, Bru?"

Brubaker shrugged. "Don't know."

"How about the weather?" suggested Walker. "I hear it's good, with scattered clouds until noon."

"No kidding? Really?" Willis caused his eyebrows to climb. "Where'd you hear that, Jack?"

"No place, but I got this trick knee, and with it I can accurately foretell the—"

"You've got fifteen minutes," said Burroughs.

"There is something I'd like to talk over," said Willis. "I want to know if we can fraternize with Martian girls or . . . if . . . I . . . I . . ." The lieutenant colonel suddenly went rigid, then began swaying in his chair. He managed to clutch his chest before toppling off his chair to the metal floor.

"Jesus, what's wrong?" Dr. Burroughs yanked his hands out of his pockets, dashed across to kneel beside the fallen astronaut. He bent close to Willis. "I can't imagine what could have happened."

"I think," said Willis, sitting up, "it must have been the toast."

Walker began laughing. Brubaker joined in.

With a straight face, Willis got up.

The doctor shook himself like a wet dog, scowling. "You guys," he said, lips close together, "are a bunch of schmucks."

"I'd like a second opinion," said Willis.

Metal bleachers had been set up a safe distance from the launch area. As the morning progressed, people began to fill the limited number of seats. They were both relatively important and very important people. Wire fencing enclosed the grandstand and military police guards patrolled the area. Several sober-faced and crew-cut Secret Service agents were also in evidence.

Representative Hollis Peaker, the heavyset chairman of the House Appropriations Committee,

9

paused behind the usher who was leading him and his wife to their seats. A pleased grin touched Peaker's broad, jowly face as he stared at the gleaming white Capricorn One rocket.

"We've reserved three of the best seats for you and Mrs. Peaker and General Enders," said the young NASA usher.

"Well, that's very thoughtful of you, son."

"In fact," the usher added, "you'll be right next to the Vice President."

"Is he here yet?"

"Not yet, sir, but he's due any minute."

"Asshole probably thinks they'll delay the launch for him," said Peaker, settling into his seat. "Somebody ought to tell him this isn't a bridge opening."

The congressman's slim wife took the seat next to him, and the grim, gray General Enders flanked her.

The young usher, with a practiced smile, handed a small leather case to Peaker and one to the general. "The agency would like you to have these commemorative binoculars," he said, "to help you to watch the launch, and as a souvenir."

"Well, thank you, son." Peaker turned the case around in his large hands. "Look here, Emily. Got the date on them and the Capricorn seal, too."

"Yes, very handsome."

"I'm glad you like them." The boy started to turn away.

Peaker caught his arm. "We'll need one more pair, son. For my wife."

"Beg pardon, sir?"

"Hollis, there's no need to fuss," the congressman's wife told him.

"We'll need another pair of these handsome binoculars, son," repeated Peaker in an even voice. "For my wife here."

"Here, Emily," offered the general, "you can take mine. Really don't need them."

"You see, congressman," explained the usher, his face slightly flushed, "there are only so many pairs of—"

"I don't believe I clearly heard you, son," Peaker said, as he smiled up at the boy. "Would you repeat that, please."

"There's no problem, sir. I'll fetch another pair right away."

Peaker nodded. "That's very thoughtful of you."

The giant red, hazy globe filled the screen.

"Good morning, everyone, this is Roy Weaver, CBS News Space Headquarters, Cape Kennedy. At this time Colonel Charles Brubaker, Lt. Colonel Peter Willis, and Commander John Walker are riding up the gantry elevator at Launch Complex 39."

The Mars slide left the television screen, replaced by a live shot of the three astronauts doing exactly what Roy Weaver said they were doing.

"They will soon be entering the giant Saturn MB V rocket," the news commentator continued. "The crew has been up for almost two hours. They had breakfast, were examined and pronounced fit. They are now preparing to embark on a four-month journey that will take them farther than any human being has ever gone. The planet Mars. And they carry with them the future of the manned-space program. This flight, as you know, comes at a time of intense pressure from a Congress that does not want to appropriate any more money to a project the public may no longer care about. It is generally agreed that if this flight is not totally successful, there will be no more support for the space program. We are a little more than two hours from lift-off. Mission Control reports everything is proceeding smoothly. CBS live color coverage will continue in one moment, after these messages."

With a surprised groan, Robert Caulfield sat upright in the rumpled bed. Rubbing his eyes he stared around the room. "Say something," he told the redhaired girl.

"Huh?"

"Say something, speak a few sentences."

"About what?"

"Anything."

"Well, this is a historic day for mankind," the girl began, tentatively, her eyes swinging between the bright TV screen and the almost awake young man in the bed. "After many long centuries of watching and waiting, man is about to embark on a flight to Mars. Soon Earthlings will set foot—"

"New Jersey," decided Caulfield. "I'm in New Jersey." He rolled out of bed. "I can tell from your accent."

"Well, I am from Jersey," the girl admitted. "Originally, I mean. But where we are is Houston, Texas."

Caulfield gave his brow a mock slap. "Texas? What am I doing in Texas?"

"Aren't you a well-known reporter? That's what you told me last night in the Longhorn Rendezvous."

Caulfield pulled up his shorts. "Right, I am a well-known reporter. Thanks for reminding me." He scanned the room again. "And this is Houston, Texas, and I'm here to cover this end of this major event." He ran his tongue over his teeth. "The problem is, all Holiday Inns are identical. You awaken in one in Houston and it's exactly like the one in Newark or Cairo."

"Have you been to Egypt?"

"I think so." He rubbed his eyes again, yawned,

ran a few fingers through his dark tangled hair. "What exactly was I drinking last night?"

"7-Up and vodka."

"Yang!" Caulfield grimaced. "No sane person would drink anything like that."

"I tried to persuade you not to last evening," the redhead said. "But you insisted if it was good enough for the Greeks, it was good enough for you."

"What Greeks?"

"The Greek truckers you were Indian wrestling with."

"Um." Caulfield's head bobbed up and down several times. He strolled toward the bathroom. "They're always in exactly the same place, bathrooms. A comforting touch in an alien and hostile land."

"Huh?"

"I am going to take a shower," he announced, "and then . . ."

She looked away from the television and at Caulfield. "And then?"

"I'm afraid I'm going to have to go to work," he said.

CHAPTER 2

THE THREE astronauts, trailed by a slightly puffing Dr. Burroughs, stepped from the gantry elevator and into the ready room. Across the small room the hatch of the capsule stood open. Three men were already in the ready room, white-clad Horace Gruning, the chief of the Rocket Firing Division, and two of his aides.

"Good morning, gentlemen," said Gruning, a chunky man in his early fifties.

"Morning, Horace," Brubaker said.

Willis, glancing around, said, "Are we late?"

"Traffic was terrible," added Walker.

Gruning smiled faintly. "I see you're all in good spirits." He was clutching a flat brown package to his chest.

"Yes, they are," said Dr. Burroughs. "I can attest to that."

"Outside of a toast-induced stroke, we're all tip-top," Willis assured him.

"Have you done the EDS tests yet?" Brubaker asked.

"They're almost complete," said Gruning.

"Do you want us to enter?"

Gruning's fingers fiddled with the paper of the package. "Yes, in a moment."

"Something?"

The brown paper tore under Gruning's fingers. "I'm not very good at things like this," he said, eyes down.

"Give it a try," urged Willis.

"I've known you . . . well, especially you, Colonel Brubaker . . . the thing is, I've known you all for some time," said Gruning, his face flushing. "What you're about to do today . . . I've spent my whole life . . ." He got the paper off the book he was clutching. "Well, I just want you to know I feel as though all I have ever worked for . . . it all has meaning today. I'm very proud today, proud of the program . . . proud of what I've been able to contribute to it in some small way. And I'm proud of you fellows." He started to hand

16

the leather-bound Bible, paused to wipe at the corner of his eye, and then gave Brubaker the book. "Anyway, I really would like you to take this Bible along with you . . . from me . . . a gift from all of us."

After a few seconds of silence Willis said, "Golly, Horace, I don't know what to say."

"Try saying nothing for a change," suggested Burroughs.

"Horace, thank you," said Brubaker, patting the Bible. "We'll be honored to take this with us."

Gruning cleared his throat. "Well, gentlemen," he said, "let's go to Mars."

"Mars?" Walker blinked. "Are you kidding? I thought we were going to Disneyland."

"Will you guys please shut up," said Burroughs, urging them toward the hatch. "Let's get started."

Brass band music flared up, more Secret Service men appeared, and then the Vice President and his wife arrived at the grandstand. The young usher escorted them to seats next to Congressman Peaker and his party.

Peaker rested his binoculars on a plump knee.

"Good morning, Mr. Vice President, and you, too, Phyllis."

"Good morning, Hollis," said Vice President Price. "Emily, General Enders." Price was a lean man, with a face that was always touched with an expression of vague perplexity.

"And how," asked Peaker, "is the President today?"

"Why, he's just fine," replied Price, smiling a vaguely perplexed smile. "He asked me to personally express his regrets for not being able to attend the launch personally. However, as you realize, there are some other matters which require his attention in Washington."

"Reelection being at the top of the list," said Peaker.

The usher held out two pairs of souvenir binoculars. "Mr. Vice President, I hope you and Mrs. Price will be very comfortable," he said. "The agency would like you both to have a pair of these commemorative binoculars."

"Why, thank you very much," said the Vice President.

A grin on his broad face, the congressman leaned toward the young man. "What's your name, son?"

"Fairfield, sir. John Fairfield."

"You learn pretty fast, you'll do all right."

"Thank you, sir."

Nodding, Peaker settled back in his chair.

"This is Paul Cunningham, Capricorn Control. We are now at T-minus 1 hour, 15 minutes and counting. Mission Control in Houston reports all systems are go, all lights are green. The weather is reported to be good, scattered clouds at five to ten thousand feet, the wind is from the east at eight knots, the sea is reported calm, with swells of less than two feet. The spacecraft is still on external power."

Zipping up her white jeans, the redhaired girl stood watching the television screen. "You're missing everything," she called toward the bathroom.

The door opened wider and steam came swirling out, followed by Caulfield. His curly black hair was less rumpled now. He had on slacks and a pale yellow shirt. "Correction, I never miss anything of importance."

"The switch to internal power will occur at T-minus 15 minutes. Colonel Brubaker has reaffirmed the completion of the EDS test checks. The launch escape system will be armed at T-minus 37 minutes. This is Capricorn Control."

"And this is Robert Caulfield, wondering where his necktie is."

The girl waved a hand toward a lamp. "You threw it over there last night."

Retrieving the tie from the lampshade, Caulfield said, "Why, I wonder, did I do such a thing?"

"After you finished doing the Latin American dance with it, you said you had no further use for it."

"Thank God I don't have total recall," said the reporter, reattaching the tie to himself.

CHAPTER 3

HARNESSED in their flight couches, the three astronauts ran through the final checkout of the maze of switches and gauges which surrounded them.

"TARS reference check," said Brubaker.

"Stage 1 is green," responded Willis.

"Stage 1 green," echoed Brubaker.

"Stage 2 is green."

"Stage 2 green."

Walker said, "Malfunction Detect System on second panel."

"Roger," said Brubaker. "MDS on second panel."

"Capricorn One, we confirm TARS and MDS," said a voice out of a speaker grid. "We have green on both. You are to go for Inertial Guidance and OAMS checks."

"Roger, Houston," said Brubaker.

From the still-open hatchway Gruning said, "Gentlemen, we are ready to shut the hatch."

"Anybody wants to get out," said Brubaker, "this is your last chance."

"One last question, Horace," said Walker. "Is Mars the red one or the green one?"

"Twenty-four billion dollars to put a wise ass in space."

"Well, it keeps me off the streets."

Making a snorting sound, Gruning closed the hatch.

The Launch Control Center in Houston was a huge room, filled with over 300 television display consoles and other computer gear. Each console was manned by a technician. On one wall a vast television screen showed the launch site in Florida. On each side of the screen were maps with a variety of colored lights which would track the orbits and flight path of the spacecraft.

Sitting unobtrusively in a relatively quiet corner of the room was Dr. James Kelloway. A thin man, with an almost gaunt face, he was fifty-three years old and the director of NASA.

From an overhead speaker came a voice. "This is Paul Cunningham, Capricorn Control. We are at T-minus 15 minutes and still counting. All systems are go, all lights are green. The flight crew has completed the final launch vehicle range safety check. Mission Control has reported the spacecraft is now on full internal power at T-minus 50 seconds."

A black colleague passed near the seated Kelloway. "A great day, Jim," he said, grinning.

Kelloway nodded, a very faint grin touching his lean face. "Yes, it is," he said in a low voice. "A great day."

"Both the Ascension and Canary tracking stations report clear reception," continued the voice on the public address system. "The prime recovery ship in the event of a terminated flight will be the U.S.S. *Kitty Hawk*, which is located 350 miles south-southeast of Bermuda. In the event of an abort before orbital insertion, the secondary recovery ship is the U.S.S. *Oriskany* in the Indian Ocean."

Very slowly Kelloway ran his tongue over his lips. And for a few seconds he let his eyes fall shut.

"Landing Module OI shutdown," announced Brubaker into his throat mike.

"Capricorn One, you should have full CM internal power."

"Roger, Houston," said Brubaker, "we have internal power."

"Vehicle final status check," said Walker.

"Begin stat—" Brubaker started to say.

Then the door of their module was opened from the outside.

CHAPTER 4

WILLIS SPOKE first. "If you're looking for the men's room, it's two doors down."

A medium-sized man in a dark business suit was standing with his head thrust into the module. Ignoring Willis, he addressed himself to Brubaker, "Bru, I'd like you and your men to please follow me."

Brubaker blinked. "Gerry, what the hell is this?"

"An emergency," replied Gerry Haig.

"What kind of an emergency?" Walker wanted to know.

"There's no time to explain. Please, just follow me now."

"This is absolutely goofy," said Brubaker. "We're about to—"

"Bru, for Christ sake, trust me," said Haig in a loud, anxious voice. "All three of you, come along. Quick!"

"I had this happen to me once in college," said Willis, while getting out of his harnesses. "All set to hop into the sack with this ample coed and then her father unexpectedly—"

"Hurry, there's very little time," Haig told them.

"This is one part of the mission we didn't rehearse." Walker moved toward the hatch. "Where exactly are we heading, Gerry?"

Haig shook his head. "Someone will explain. The urgent thing now is to get the hell out of here."

"Just when I was starting to like the neighborhood," remarked Willis.

"This is Paul Cunningham, Capricorn Control. We are coming up on T-minus 5 minutes and counting. The space vehicle final checks have been completed. The access arm is swinging into a full retreat position. This means the destruct system is now fully armed."

"TLR pressure reading is 45 point 2."

"Roger, Houston. 45 point 2."

A door on the back side of the gantry swung open. Hidden from the view of the launch spectators, the three astronauts emerged, led by Haig. A van was waiting at the exit, back doors hanging open.

"In here, quick," urged Haig.

Brubaker stopped short. "Will you, damn it, tell us what in the—"

"In, in, for Christ sake." Haig grabbed Brubaker's arm and hustled him up into the back of the van.

"I feel like we're one step ahead of a lynch mob," said Walker as he somewhat reluctantly followed Brubaker into the shadows of the van.

When the three astronauts were inside with Haig, he shut the doors and locked them. The van made a skidding U-turn and went roaring away.

"This is Paul Cunningham, Capricorn Control. We are at T-minus 3 minutes, 6 seconds. The launch officer has given a go to begin the Firing Command Automatic Sequence. From now until T-minus 50 seconds the system is preset. At T-minus 50 seconds the launch vehicle will be on full internal power, which begins the actual launch sequence. All systems are go, all lights are green."

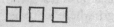

The copter's blades were chopping at the air as it sat on the landing strip. The van came to a jerking halt near it. Haig came out first, brushing at wrinkles in his trousers. "Right over here now, Bru," he said, motioning to the other astronauts. "We want all of you in the chopper."

Brubaker eased out of the van and stopped when he was facing Haig.

"We're not going any farther, Gerry, until you—"

"Listen, Bru," said Haig, after an anxious glance at the waiting helicopter, "you have to trust me. Believe me when I tell you I am not crazy. We all have your best interests at heart."

"Our best interests are in that damn rocket," said Walker, angry, joining Brubaker on the strip.

Haig was breathing through his mouth, his head ticking slightly from side to side. "I'm acting on Kelloway's orders, for Christ sake."

28

Ambling up to them, Willis asked, "Why would Kelloway order us to do a damn fool thing like this?"

"I'll let him tell you that himself," said Haig. "Now for the love of God, get into this damn ship."

Willis, an eyebrow raised, looked at Brubaker. "What do we do, chief?"

Brubaker lowered his head for a few seconds. Raising it, he said, "I guess we go wherever it is they want us to go and see what Kelloway has to say."

"Right, that's the best thing to do," said Haig, urging them over to the helicopter.

The trio of astronauts were soon inside the copter. Haig hurried back to the van. He didn't stay to watch the copter climb into the sky.

CHAPTER 5

SMOKE BEGAN to pour from the bottom of Capricorn One.

"7 . . . 6 . . . 5 . . . we have outboard engines . . . 4 . . . 3 . . . we have inboard engines . . . 2 . . . 1 . . . 0 . . ."

The launch pad was filled with glaring flame. The rocket roared and began to lift.

"We have launch commit . . . we have a lift-off . . . we have a lift-off!"

For a few flaming instants the rocket seemed to hover. Then it began to rise and rise.

Dr. Kelloway placed his forefinger on the bridge

of his glasses, pushed them a fraction down his nose, then up again. He turned away from the huge screen in the Mission Control center and stopped watching the rocket's ascent for a moment.

"Looking good, Capricorn," came an amplified voice.

"Roger, Houston, we are starting yaw," said a voice that was Brubaker's.

Kelloway couldn't seem to get the glasses exactly where he wanted them. He finally took them off entirely.

People were leaving the grandstand. Congressman Peaker, very carefully holding his souvenir binoculars, said to the Vice President, "Well, everything went perfectly, didn't it? Lift-off, separation. Beautiful."

"Very impressive, yes." The Vice President rose from his chair.

"NASA's got a few more impressive tricks up its sleeve."

"No doubt, Hollis."

With a moderate grunt, the heavyset congressman lifted himself out of his seat. "You'll be sure and give my regards to the President?"

31

"I'll be glad to."

"I do hope that whatever matters kept him from being here," said Peaker, moving his thick face close to the other man's, "will be successfully dealt with."

"That's very thoughtful of you, Hollis. The President, I'm sure, will be most pleased to learn of your support."

"He might receive a little more of my support if he'd be a shade more helpful to the program here."

"Now, you know how interested he is in the space program."

"Interest and support," said the congressman, "aren't the same thing."

"There are a lot of people, Hollis," the Vice President told him, "who believe we have some problems here on Earth which merit our attention. So before we spend more billions on outer space, we ought to make some improvements a bit closer to home."

"And there are also people who think our most important problem is our declining position as a world leader."

Vice President Price gave the congressman the briefest of pats on the arm and then turned away, saying, "It's been nice seeing you again, Hollis."

"Likewise, Mr. Vice President."

The astronauts were transferred from the helicopter to a military Falcon jet. Two men in civilian clothes hurried them into the plane, escorted them into the passenger compartment, and left them there. A moment later the jet took off.

"This isn't," said Walker, "the kind of trip I was planning for today."

Brubaker seated himself as best he could in his gear. "Maybe I shouldn't admit this, fellas," he said slowly, "but so far I'm pretty much baffled."

"Well, in the words of that great philosopher," said Willis, "we might as well relax and enjoy it."

CHAPTER 6

     "THE MIDDLE of nowhere," observed Walker as he came down the disembark ramp of the jet.

There was only a glaring yellow desert all around them. It was absolutely flat, giving off a wavery haze. The only building visible anywhere was the huge hangar they'd landed near. The only signs of life were the two crew-cut, dark-suited men who were waiting on the hot runway.

"Didn't Beau Geste used to live around here?" inquired Willis.

One of the crew-cut young men approached Bru-

34

baker. "How do you do, Colonel," he said in a crisp, polite voice. "Will you please come along this way."

Brubaker shook his head and put his hands on his hips. He and the other two astronauts were wearing only their white jump suits now. "Not going any damn place," he assured his new guide, "until somebody tells us what the hell is going on."

"Everything will be explained to you inside," said the man.

"Bullshit! I want to know now, right now."

The second man said, "If we were in a position, Colonel Brubaker, to explain things, we most certainly would. If you'll just be patient enough to come inside with us, I promise you'll soon understand."

"Are we kidnapped?"

The other man brushed at his crew cut. "I know this sounds strange, but we're all working for the same thing," he said. "Really. You'll understand this whole business, when you come inside."

"Maybe we better go inside, Bru," said Walker.

"Doesn't look like we got a hell of a lot of choice," Brubaker said. He gave his guides a mock salute. "Lead on!"

Willis scrutinized the hangar while they walked toward it. "Can't say I care much for the color scheme," he decided. "Painted the same color as this grungy desert. You know what I think, Jack?"

"What, boss?"

"I think this joint's meant to be camouflaged."

One of the crew-cut young men opened a metal door. He ushered the astronauts into a chilly metal corridor. Footfalls echoed with a tinny sound.

The first crew-cut young man halted and opened a metal door, which led off the corridor. "If you'll wait in here for a few moments . . ."

The room had white metal walls, no windows. Several functional metal chairs ringed a formica table.

"Heck of a way to come just for a poker game," said Willis.

When the three astronauts were inside, the door was closed on them.

"No cards," said Walker, nodding at the bare table. "What this reminds me of is the waiting room of a doctor's office. You think they could have found out I got the clap?"

"There's an idea," said Willis, eying a chair for awhile before finally sitting in it. "They probably don't want to give all the Martians a dose. You should have told them."

"Let's be serious for a moment," suggested Brubaker.

"We are serious. We don't want all the Martians coming down with a social disease," said Willis, rocking in his straight chair and clasping his hands behind his head. "Wouldn't that give the space program a black eye?"

Brubaker paced. "I can't figure this mess out at all."

"Red China," said Walker. "It's a Red Chinese plot."

"I favor Blue Chinese," said Willis. "They go better with the decor."

The door opened. All three men turned to stare at Dr. Kelloway. He hesitated on the threshold, then came in and shut the door behind him. "Good morning."

"Hi there, doc," said Willis, watching the NASA director seat himself at the head of the table. "A funny thing happened on the way to Mars."

Brubaker's nostrils flared. "This isn't a goddamn tea party, Jim," he said. "So cut the shit and tell us what's going on!"

"Everybody sit down, okay?" Kelloway ran his tongue over his upper lip, his eyes never quite meeting theirs.

Walker, after a glance at Brubaker, sat.

Brubaker stayed where he was.

"This isn't exactly easy for me either," said Kelloway, sighing.

"Well, that's tough shit," said Brubaker.

Another sigh. "Okay, here it is," said Kelloway, watching his hands press into the table top. "I guess I better start by telling you that if there was any other way, even a slight chance of some alternative, I'd give anything not to be here with you at this moment. Anything!" He forced himself to look directly at the two seated men in turn, then up at Brubaker. "Bru, how long have we known each other?"

"I'd have to check my diary."

"I wish you wouldn't be . . . sixteen years. Right, that's how long we've been friends," said Kelloway, his head lowered again. "Boy, you should have seen yourself then. You looked like you'd just stepped off a Wheaties box. When I'd told everybody about this dream I had of conquering the biggest damn new frontier there was . . . well, most of them looked at me like I was nuts. But not you, Bru. You looked at me and you said, 'Okay, when?'" Kelloway's left hand grasped his right. "I remember the talks we had about making this a better world, by finding out about other worlds. We were going to reach so high. . . . In school, in college, I never had that many . . . close friends. I guess I made up for it with you, got all the missed bull sessions out of my system." He risked a glance at Brubaker. "I remember when you told me Kay was pregnant the first time. We went out and got crocked. Then when Charlie was born, we got crocked again. The two of us, Flash Gordon and Dr. Zarkov, talking about reaching the distant stars, and the bartender telling us we'd had enough. Then

Armstrong stepped out on the moon and we cried, because we were so proud. Willis, you and Walker came in around then. Both bright and talented wise asses who—"

"Maybe this is doing something for you, Jim," said Brubaker, striding up to the table. "But I could do with a lot less hearts and flowers and a few more hard, cold facts about why the hell you grabbed us out of Capricorn One and dragged us here. Wherever the hell here is."

Kelloway raised a hand, almost as though he were afraid his long-time friend was going to hit him. "Believe me, Bru, honest to God, this is one of the toughest things I've ever had to do," he said. "Let me, please, work up to it my way."

Walker gave a nod. "Let him speak his piece, Bru."

Snorting out his breath, Brubaker took hold of a chair, turned it around and straddled it. "Okay, okay, let's hear the whole spiel."

"I remember when Glenn made his first orbit in Mercury. Christ, they put up TV sets in Grand Central Station. Thousands of commuters missed their trains to watch," said Kelloway. "But when Apollo 17 landed on the moon, people called up the networks to bitch because the reruns of *I Love Lucy* were preempted. Lucy, for Christ sake, and her broken-English husband meant more to them than one of the major achievements of civilization." He

39

twisted his fingers and sank lower in his chair. "And the presidents, my God. They'd dislocate their jaws praising the space program. Then, I don't know exactly why, all you began to hear was how much it was all costing. Is it worth 20 billion to go to another planet? Why not a cure for cancer? Why not rebuild the slums? As though you could use cost accounting on a dream." He separated his hands, placed them flat on the formica. "And today. Who was at the launch. The Veep. That prissy bastard and his dimwit wife. The President was too busy. Yeah, too busy and a little bit chicken-shit. Two months ago he told me, 'Jim, make this one good. Congress is on my back. They're looking for a reason to cancel the whole program. You can't afford one single screw-up. This one has to be perfect, or it's all over.' All over. The only way he'd even agreed to make the phone call to Mars during the landing was when I told him he could make it collect."

Brubaker leaned forward. "I still don't get it."

"You will, bear with me. I'm sorry I have to just about preach a sermon to you guys," said Kelloway. "What I'm working up to is, the President—hail to the chief—the damn President of the United States, made it perfectly clear to me that we could not afford a screw-up." He raised his hands, then let them fall. "So guess what, gents? We had a screw-up. Yeah, a first-class, bona fide, made-in-the-USA screw-up."

"Nobody told us," said Walker.

"The nice people from Con Amalgamate delivered us a life-support system cheap enough to allow them a nice profit on the deal," continued Kelloway. "That's okay, the profit motive. What makes the wheels turn. Except this time there was just a little too much profit and not enough life support. We found out two months ago it won't work. You guys would all be dead in a shade under three weeks. Simple as that. Now you might think all I had to do was make a nice report. 'Excuse it, Mr. President, we got us a little screw-up.' Sure, and then Congress has a perfect excuse. The President gets off the hook, and we go no more a-roving. One foul-up too many, goodbye space program. What's so important about Mars anyway?" He took a deep breath, pushed at the table and stood up. "Well, that's the speech. Now I'd like you to come along with me." He walked to the door without waiting for them.

CHAPTER 7

THERE was Mars.

Its dry, rocky surface a red-orange. And there was the Capricorn One Landing Module standing wide-legged on that alien ground.

Kelloway crossed the sound stage and stepped onto the red dust of Mars. He halted, then beckoned to the three astronauts. "Come on, this is what I wanted to show you," he said.

Brubaker went first. Walking very slowly, taking it all in. The huge grid-ceilinged room, the watching television cameras, the panorama of space painted meticulously on a cyclorama, the exact replica of the Command Module suspended nearby.

"Tell me this isn't what I think it is, Jim," he said.

Kelloway was looking across the glowing Martian landscape, eyes narrowed as he signaled to someone in a glass-faced booth which sat in the shadows. "Want you to hear something, Bru."

Voices came from a speaker concealed in the shadowy cross beams.

"Your system analysis looks good, for TMI."

"Roger, Houston," came Brubaker's voice, "TMI burn time will be 5 minutes, 45 seconds."

"Capricorn One, 5:45 is correct. Carnavon advises you are in tracking."

"Roger, Houston."

"What did you do," asked Walker, joining them, "send up Rich Little instead of us?"

Brubaker said, "You don't think you're really going to get away with this?"

With a sad shrug Kelloway said, "Don't know. But it's a chance. Probably not a very good one, but the only chance we've got."

"Who knows about this?"

"As few people as possible," answered Kelloway. "Houston is monitoring the actual flight. All the telemetry is coming from the Command Module. So are your voices and medical data. We recorded everything from the practice simulations. So Houston doesn't know." He paused, rubbed his hands over the front of his coat. "All we need from you is the actual television transmissions during the flight and the Mars landing. That's all."

"Oh, that's all? We parade around on this . . . this phony movie set and pretend we really went to Mars!"

"If there's one thing we know how to do, Bru, it's construct a realistic and convincing mock-up of the surface of Mars. Believe me, this one will look completely believable on camera."

"Unless," said Walker, "one of your goons walks through it on the way to the john or something."

Kelloway said, "We inserted a change in the on-board computer, so the spacecraft will land two hundred miles off target when it returns to Earth. You guys'll be flown to an island near that point. From there you'll be transferred to a chopper. The copter flies you to the capsule and you'll be put inside. It should take the recovery forces a minimum of an hour and a half to reach the splashdown site. When the prime recovery carrier arrives, they'll take you out of the spacecraft."

"Golly, you thought of everything," observed Walker.

"I don't know, Jack, but I hope so."

"And you're sure we'll just go along with this, huh?" asked Brubaker.

"No, I'm not. Not at all."

"What if we say no."

"I don't know," said Kelloway slowly. "Don't say no."

Willis said, "When does Allen Funt come in and tell us we're on Candid Camera?"

"Jesus, do you think I like this?" said Kelloway, turning toward him. "You think I want to admit I'm really standing here telling you all this crazy crap about patching in tape recordings and sneaking you guys back into an empty craft? It's just that . . . I care so damned much that I think it's all worth it. Well, no, I'm not even sure of that."

"We participate in a momentous con job," said Brubaker. "What does that do for anybody?"

"Damn it, Bru, it will keep something alive that shouldn't die," said Kelloway. "I really think we're important to the country, that we've meant something. Now we're . . . it's like being on the edge of a cliff and just hanging on by your fingernails. If you back out, well, it gives a lot of decent people one less good thing to believe in."

Brubaker laughed. "What kind of horseshit are you handing out, Jim? We go along with this crazy thing, we lie our asses off. And somehow the world of truth and ideals and beauty is protected." He shook his head. "If we don't take part in this super rip-off of yours, then we're supposed to be the bad guys. I don't buy it, Jim. Though I have to admire your gall in trying it out on us."

"You're twisting my words around, Bru."

"Listen, Jim," said Brubaker, putting a hand on the man's shoulder. "I don't see all this quite as you do. I'm not so sure that canceling a flight or cutting off appropriations, for that matter, is going to mean America folds up."

"You're trying to make me sound like some kind of simplistic Washington idiot," complained Kelloway. "You know me better than that."

"Thought I did."

Walker said, "Listen, if the only way to keep something alive is to become a liar, then I don't think it's worth keeping alive."

"Please," Kelloway said to all of them, "you have to help. Don't you understand, you *have* to!"

"What the hell does that mean?" demanded Brubaker, taking his hand off Kelloway and stepping back. "What do you mean we *have* to?"

"You have to," said Kelloway in a low voice.

"What if we don't?"

"Please, Bru. Please. Don't put me in a corner."

"You're crazy," shouted Brubaker. "You are absolutely one hundred percent out of your frigging mind, Jim! You've got us standing here in the middle of this nuthouse and you're worried about being put in a corner. Jesus H. Christ!"

"Your families," murmured Kelloway, head down.

Brubaker took hold of both the man's shoulders this time. "What did you say?"

"Your families," repeated the NASA director, eyes downcast.

"What about our families?"

"Please, just help me and we—"

"What about our families?" Brubaker shook him hard, then let him go.

Kelloway stumbled and fell over. Red Martian dust went swirling up. "This thing is out of my hands," he said, getting up. "You may think it's just a couple of goofy scientists who don't know when to throw in the towel. But it isn't, Bru." He brushed himself off. "There are people out there, forces out there. They have a lot to lose. They're grown-ups, and they're playing grown-up rules."

"What about our families?" said Walker.

"They're flying back," said Kelloway. "Jesus, this isn't my idea. But . . . they're all on the plane between the Cape and Houston. All together, you know, on the plane."

Brubaker started to reach for Kelloway, then let his hands drop and stood staring at him. "You're not serious, Jim?"

"Don't make me go on with this, Bru. Just . . . please . . . say yes."

"Tell me! Tell me, you crazy son of a bitch!"

Kelloway took in a hesitant breath. "Okay,

they're on the plane. There's a device on the plane with them," he said. "There are these people, powerful people. If I don't give them the all-clear signal by a certain time, they'll explode the device. Can't you understand this? I didn't mean for it to get out of control, but it is."

"Jim, you couldn't," said Brubaker. "You couldn't do anything like that."

"I have to," answered Kelloway.

CHAPTER 8

SHE NEVER took the window seat. It was ridiculous, probably, but she felt safer on the aisle. Kay Brubaker was a pretty woman in her middle thirties, dark-haired, and a shade plump. She was sitting in the jet, which was taking them home to Houston. Next to her, in the window seat, Janet Willis was chatting away.

"Yes, I know," Kay said now and then, not really aware of what the blonde was saying.

This was going to be a very difficult time, and it was only just starting. Days and days to go yet, with Bru out there. Very difficult, but she'd do it.

Fill the time, take care of the kids, smile at friends, be sweet to the press. So long as they couldn't see inside her, it was okay.

"You feeling all right, Kay?"

"What?"

"You look sort of pale," observed Janet.

Kay realized she was clutching her hands together, that her fingers had a pinched, bloodless look. "Don't tell anybody, it'd be bad for public relations," she said, "but I'm nervous as hell."

"So am I," admitted Janet. "I find if you keep talking away, about any old thing, it helps."

"I think maybe I'm too nervous for much in the way of small talk."

"You know," said Janet, "I used to be afraid of flying. But I got to thinking, compared to what Pete is going through, why, a ride in a jet is nothing. It's no more dangerous than crossing the street."

"I've almost been hit three times, crossing the street," said Kay.

Bob Caulfield eased down, uninvited, into a chair. He flashed a brief grin at the pretty blonde across the restaurant table. He picked up the menu, studied it, muttering to himself. Snapping it shut, he said, "Mind if I join you?"

"Yes," said Judy Drinkwater. "It would ruin my whole day, not to mention my appetite."

"I'm having, Judy, somewhat of a problem with a hangover," he confided. "Usually if I drink a little of what I had the night before, it cures me. I'm informed, by reliable sources, that last evening I was seen consuming 7-Up and vodka, and so far I can't bring myself to—"

"Why don't you take a flying leap, Bob?"

"You think that would help my hangover?"

Judy leaned forward, resting her hands on the crisp white tablecloth. "Buzz off."

Caulfield sighed. "You're letting this network rivalry thing foul up your otherwise excellent judgment," he told the girl. "You work for CBS and I labor for NBC. That's not exactly a Montague-Capulet set-up."

"I wouldn't like you if you were Walter Cronkite's long-lost brother."

"Gee, Judy, after the good times we had together in Lisbon I thought—"

"I was never in Lisbon with you."

Caulfield snapped his fingers. "Darn, that's right. It was that other stunning blonde who works for CBS. I'm always getting you two mixed—"

"That's another thing that's loathsome about you, this offensive macho act of yours. You're always implying that you've laid every girl from here to Timbuktu."

"No, actually I couldn't get anywhere with the one in Timbuktu." Caulfield picked up the menu again. "Since you loathe me, Judy, I think I'll ask for separate checks. Okay?"

CHAPTER 9

HE WAS wondering if he had the flu—some new kind, maybe. He felt a little odd, somewhat disoriented. Elliot Whitter, a modest-sized young man, sat slightly hunched over his read-out monitor in the vast Mission Control room in Houston.

On the large television screen on the far wall, only a test pattern showed.

"This is Paul Cunningham, Capricorn Control. We are at T-plus 2 days, 4 hours, 31 minutes into the flight. Some 9 hours since TMI. The Command Module is still linked with the Landing Module, on top of the S-4B third stage. At T-plus 2 days, 4 hours, 32 minutes Lt. Colonel Willis will activate the on-board television camera. That should be in about 30 seconds. In 3 minutes Colonel Brubaker will detach the Command Module from the S-4B, turning it around so it faces the Landing Module and then perform a docking maneuver. After that the Command and Landing Modules will jettison the S-4B. We're coming up on T-plus 2 days, 4 hours, 32 minutes."

The test pattern snapped off the giant screen and was replaced by crackling snow.

"Capricorn One, this is Houston."

"Roger, Houston," came Brubaker's voice.

"We have hash."

"We're turning the camera on now."

Wavy lines took over the screen.

"We have transmission, Capricorn One."

A picture formed. There were Brubaker, Willis, and Walker, strapped into their couches.

"How is it?" asked Brubaker.

"We have a good picture now."

"Roger, Houston."

Willis said, "CSM on nominal azimuth."

"Houston," said Brubaker, "we're ready for CSM-S-4B separation."

"We read you, Capricorn. You are to go for separation."

Elliot Whitter frowned. He rubbed a palm over

his forehead. It didn't seem too warm, so maybe it wasn't the flu, although there were strains of flu where you didn't run a fever. He shook his head, blinked and again studied the digits on his screen. He leaned back in his chair and glanced around the room, ignoring the maneuvers which were taking place on the wall screen.

Whitter punched out another sequence on his keyboard. Numbers flashed across his small screen.

He raised his hand to his mouth and coughed. Even if he was on the brink of the flu, he knew he wasn't seeing things.

Whitter bit his lip. He leaned back in his chair, unhitched his headset, and again glanced around the room.

"Roger, Capricorn. It looks good here. The flight director advises you are to go for landing."

"Inspection complete," said Walker.

"Inspection complete. Well done, Capricorn."

The big wall screen went black. You could feel relaxation spread through the room. The people manning the monitors let themselves ease back. There was a scatter of conversation.

Whitter nodded his head twice and got out of his chair. He walked along an aisle of monitors and up to another level.

Dr. Bergen was a tall, gray-haired man in a conservative blue suit. He was standing and watching the darkened wall screen when Whitter tapped his arm. "Elliot, yes?"

"Uh," said Whitter, "I'd like to talk to you, Dr. Bergen."

"Fine, what is it?"

Whitter gestured back at his monitor. "Um . . . well, there's something I . . . something . . ."

"Are you ill, Elliot?"

"Well, I think maybe I've got a bug or something," said Whitter, "but that's not the problem, doctor. It's my read-out."

Bergen's eyes narrowed. "What about the read-out, Elliot?"

"Well, I can't figure something out."

"Maybe I can help you."

"Well, sir, I was running a check on my own," explained Whitter, "on the transmission signals."

"On your own?" Dr. Bergen rubbed his chin. "Well, that's dedication."

"Now, sir, on the read-out," said Whitter, "well, the television signals are coming in ahead of the spacecraft signals. It's like they're closer, much closer."

"That's not possible, Elliot," said Bergen. "There must be a malfunction in your equipment. Either that or the fact that you're feeling a little fuzzy."

Whitter shook his head. "I don't think so, Dr. Bergen," said Whitter. "And to make sure I wasn't off, I double-checked the console by—"

"Which console are you on?"

"It's 36, sir."

"Well, there's the answer." Bergen patted him on the shoulder. "We've been having some problems with the circuitry on 36."

"No one told me."

"We should have, Elliot. And I'll make sure it's repaired at once," Bergen assured him. "Meanwhile, why don't you take the rest of the day off. See if you can shake the bug, okay?" Another pat on the shoulder. "Thanks for telling me about the problem. It shows a real initiative that I like. Bye now." He turned and walked away.

Whitter watching him, slowly shaking his head. "It's not me," he said. "And, damn it, it's not the console."

CHAPTER 10

WALKER RELEASED the restraining straps on his couch. He pushed down gently on the couch and seemed to float weightlessly upward. The black man kept his arms outstretched, gingerly fending off the protruding surfaces of the Command Module as he rose. Walker concentrated on his performance, making sure he gave no hint that he was actually being pulled upward by unseen cables attached to hydraulic winches in the scaffolding of the sound stage. It was tough, harder than the real thing would have been.

"Houston," said Brubaker, "Landing Module depressurization is green here."

"We read green here," responded Houston.

"I see the hatch here," said Walker. "I'm going to open it."

"Roger, you are to go to open."

The winches did their work as Walker rose higher and out of the picture that was being transmitted on television sets across the country.

"I have the hatch, Houston," he said, avoiding a glance up at the two men in the rafters who were operating the winches.

"Roger, Capricorn."

"I am pulling the LM depressurization rings."

"Roger, Capricorn," came the voice from Houston. "You are to go to open LM hatch."

Walker gave the hatch one complete clockwise rotation, and it opened downward. "Hatch open."

"Looks good."

Walker took hold of the sides of the hatch opening and tugged. He hoped like hell none of the damn cables would get tangled. It had all worked fine in the rehearsal, but this was for real. He was going to look awfully silly if something went blooey at this point.

But nothing did. The illusion was maintained, and he seemed to float, without weight, up into the Landing Module.

"I'm in the LM, Houston."

"How does it look?"

"Everything looks nominal. CRL lights are green," recited Walker. "OAMS panel is on."

"We read 55 minutes of RCS fuel," said Willis down in the Command Module. Willis made a notation on his slate and then let go of the pencil. It seemed to float up level with his shoulder. Willis caught it, careful not to touch the wire it was dangling from.

"55 minutes here," said Walker.

"We copy 55 minutes," said Houston. "That is 5 minutes better than nominal."

"LM is functional," announced Walker.

"Roger, Capricorn. It looks good here. The flight director advises you to go for a landing."

"I'm coming back. Inspection complete."

"Inspection complete. You may return. Well done, Capricorn."

The lights on the TV camera went off and Walker came thumping down into his couch. "You sure 'Space Cadet' started this way?"

"Very convincing performance," said Willis, tossing his pencil into the air and watching it dangle. "You're a credit to your race, Jack, old man."

"Shit," said Walker.

CHAPTER 11

A PLEASANT residential block, clean-cut and bright, like a good many others in this quiet suburb of Houston. Except this particular block was packed at the moment with mobile television units, police cars and even a snack wagon. Cameramen, reporters, and technicians filled the streets in front of the house, awaiting the emergence of Kay Brubaker.

Bob Caulfield, clutching a freshly acquired plastic cup of coffee, lowered himself to the curb and sat. Glancing to his right, he said, "Fancy meeting you here."

Judy Drinkwater said, "Go spritz up a rope."

Caulfield gave a hollow chuckle. "Very good, Judy, pretending to dislike me. No use letting all these other turkeys know how deeply we feel about each other. None of ABC's business, or PBS' or—"

"How come you didn't shave this morning?"

"I always shave, I'm always immaculately groomed, Judy. Around the corridors of NBC I'm known as Dapper Bob." He rubbed tentatively at his cheek. "Didn't stand close enough to the razor this morning. Buzzing unsettles me."

"More macho propaganda," remarked Judy, taking a sip of coffee.

"How terrible is the coffee?"

"Not too."

"Bet it's godawful."

"Don't drink it, then."

"Aw, I'm no good without my morning coffee," Caulfield said. "I wager this stuff isn't even as good as what they give out free to flood victims." After some preliminary fiddling he got the plastic lid off his cup. "Everything has to be unwrapped or opened."

"Um," said Judy.

"Seems like I'm always unwrapping things. Wake up, take the cellophane off the drinking glass, take that funny waxy paper off the Holiday Inn soap. Even my toilet has a paper band over it, to tell me I'm the first one to sit on it this time around. A virgin toilet. I have a fear that if I stay in the sack too long, they'll come in and wrap me up in Saran Wrap."

"Poor Bob."

"No, but I'm serious. After awhile you forget what city you're in. It could be Houston or Cincinnati or Cairo. Everything is the same, including most of the people. There's got to be a factory, someplace secret, where they turn out Holiday Inn waitresses."

"Maybe you ought to get into another line of work. A cousin of mine started a chicken ranch out in Petaluma and he—"

"No, Judy, this is my calling, my life's work," said Caulfield. "What I'm saying is things would be a lot more endurable if I were going through this with someone I cared about, someone who could share all these dehumanizing things with me, someone to stand by my—"

"Bullshit!"

"That's not the response I was building for."

"You need a new act, Robert. This one is so old, I think you've even pulled it on me before."

"Act?" He struck at his chest with his free hand rolled into a fist. "What's that supposed to mean?"

"Well, there was Liz Haller in California, during the primary out there. You did the plastic society business with her, plus your both being witnesses to the unfolding-of-history bit."

Caulfield gave a lopsided shrug. "It worked."

"Lot of goofy things work in California."

"But really, Judy, I'm sincere with you. I honestly feel—"

"Bullshit, if you'll forgive my repeating myself."

"You wouldn't know sincerity if it ran over you."

"Not if you were driving it."

Caulfield gazed heavenward. "Why, Lord, did I have to fall in love with a wise-ass broad?"

"It's probably because we're both witnesses to history unfolding," suggested the blonde.

"I give up." Caulfield tried his coffee. "Yang!"

"Don't give up so easily. Just change your approach."

"Oh, so?" Carefully he dumped the coffee into the gutter. "What sort of approach would you suggest?"

"You ought to be a lot more direct . . . and honest," Judy told him. "I admire a guy who simply comes out and says, 'Hey I'd like to screw you!' "

"You think that would work?"

"Stands a better chance than the stuff about sharing a meaningful life together."

"Okay," said Caulfield. "I'd like to screw you."

"Go screw yourself."

A modest commotion commenced around them. Cameramen scrambled to their feet, reporters grabbed their mikes. The front door of the house had opened and Kay Brubaker had stepped out into the morning.

Caulfield bounded over to his soundman and retrieved his microphone. "Good morning, Mrs. Brubaker."

Another newsman asked, "How are you feeling?"

"Are you excited?"

"Do you get much sleep?"

"I'm sorry you have to wait outside the house like this so much," Kay began. "There's not much I can say, except that, yes, I am very excited. Everything seems to be going very smoothly, for which I'm very thankful. Dr. Kelloway called me to tell me Bru and the crew are in excellent spirits."

"How has all this," asked Judy, "disrupted your family routine?"

Near the girl's ear Caulfield murmured, "That's a brilliant question."

Judy jabbed him in the vicinity of the heart with her elbow. "Not as sparkling as your 'Good morning, Mrs. Brubaker,' but not bad."

". . . the children will continue to go to school," Kay was saying. "We'll try as hard as we can to have a normal life. Now, if you'll excuse me, I have to get back inside. I just came out to say hello to all of you, and to thank you for being so very patient."

CHAPTER 12

THEY WERE a team, Kay Brubaker thought, like their husbands. A set. See one, you expect to see the other two. So here they all were, side by side. Kay in the middle, with Janet Willis on her right and Liz Walker on her left, wearing their Capricorn One visitor badges. Trying to look brave, not nervous, and all the time wondering and worrying. So many things might go wrong. You never let that show, never let anyone see you had doubts.

Out in the vast Control Center room, on the other side of the glass booth window, you could sense excitement. Even though people were doing their jobs, tending their consoles, doing whatever else it was they had to do. Bru had tried to explain all the technical stuff to her, and she'd read about it. In interviews Kay was able to give the impression she was a very well-informed astronaut's wife. There were, though, things she couldn't understand, some she'd simply forgotten.

There was Jim Kelloway out on the floor. He sensed Kay was looking at him, turned, and gave her that small grin and guarded wave which were so characteristic of him. What was he thinking inside? What was he feeling? Did he have any of the doubts or fears she felt?

"This is Paul Cunningham, Capricorn Control. We are at T-plus 131 days, 4 hours 15 minutes into the flight. The flight director reports that all is going well. The Landing Module has been successfully checked and the crew is in excellent health."

Janet pressed Kay's hand. They watched the giant TV screen, which still showed only the test pattern.

"In just a few moments we should be receiving a television signal from the spacecraft. It is important to know that it takes 21 minutes for the signal from Mars to reach Earth. We have no way of communicating with Capricorn One, and what we'll be seeing actually happened 21 minutes ago."

The screen went black.

"We have no signal from Capricorn One."

There was the crackle of static.

"We are getting something."

"Houston, this is Capricorn One. Houston, this is Capricorn One," came Brubaker's voice.

Kay realized she'd been holding her breath. She sighed it out.

"CM/LM separation was nominal. I have CM in visual contact through port window. Delta-V burn time 2 point 3 seconds."

"3 point 3 second burn is correct. We should hear from the CM soon."

"Houston, this is Capricorn CM." It was Willis' voice.

Kay squeezed Janet's hand.

"I see the Landing Module. I have him 22 degrees starboard."

"He will now inspect undercarriage."

"I see the undercarriage. Houston, it looks good."

"They will start Descent Orbital Initiation. DOI time should be 4 minutes, 35 seconds."

"We are starting DOI," announced Brubaker.

Congressman Peaker was happy. He sipped at his coffee and beamed across his desk at the large color television set which filled one corner of his Washington office. Five other men were gathered in the office—two aides and three fellow congressmen.

"You wait," he said. "In about five minutes that asshole Price is going to call and tell me how pleased the President is."

On his color screen the red surface of Mars showed.

"This is Paul Cunningham, Capricorn Control. The flight director advises that the LM crew has been given a go for the first EVA on the Martian surface. Because the time delay would make a conversation impossible, the crew has taken a prerecorded message from the President of the United States along with them. When they are on the Martian surface, Commander Walker will activate the recorder and the crew will hear the message for the first time."

"Houston," came Brubaker's voice, "I have the hatch."

"Camera activated," said Walker.

Fully suited and helmeted, Brubaker emerged from the spindly legged module. He gingerly lowered himself out of the hatch and down the ladder. Halting on the final step, he said, "I'm on the bottom step."

Peaker chuckled. His aides chuckled.

Poised on the bottom step, his booted foot still

not touching the red surface of Mars, Brubaker said, "I take this step in the journey of peace for all mankind."

He left the step and seemed to float to the ground.

"Houston, I am on the surface of Mars."

While Brubaker bounced on the surface of the planet, Walker descended the stairs and joined him.

The two men joined each other, then unfurled an American flag. Sticking the small metal flagpole firmly into the ground, Brubaker said, "We do not claim this planet in the name of America. We claim it in the name of all the people of the planet Earth. We hope that our visits will increase the understanding of the human race."

"Houston," said Walker, "I am starting the tape." Walker had moved to the module. He rejoined Brubaker and stood beside him.

"To the men of Capricorn One," began the recorded voice of the President, "I bring you greetings from your fellow Americans. And from, I am sure, all the citizens of the world. There are moments in history when an event occurs which unites all people. When the Second World War broke out, all free men and women—black, white, British, Russian—put aside their differences and realized we were partners in a civilization that goes beyond our geographic borders."

"The asshole is almost eloquent," remarked Peaker. "Has he got a new writer?"

"Wrote this himself," said one of the other congressmen. "So I hear."

"No shit?"

"Now you three men, with your courage, optimism, and strength, have brought all of us together again. We will never be the same. For this moment, more than any moment in our history, has made all the people in the world realize we are part of a planet, which is part of a system which is part of a universe. We are a small, energetic species, capable of pettiness, yet capable of brilliance. You have shown us how wonderful we can be, by showing us how high we can reach. You have crossed the last great frontier. You have shown us we are people of different colors, religions, and ideologies, but a single people nonetheless. You are the basic truth in us, you are our reality. We will never let you down, and we will always be grateful."

After a second the phone on Peaker's wide desk rang.

The plump congressman answered it. "Yes? Ah, hello there, Mr. Vice President." He winked at the others in his office. "Yes, it is. Yes, it's wonderful, Mr. Vice President. A very proud and wonderful moment for all Americans. I see, yes. Well, you be sure to tell the President that's very gracious of him. I appreciate it, I really do. Thank you, and my best to you and your lovely wife. Yes, goodbye." Peaker hung up and took another sip of his coffee. "Asshole."

After a moment of hesitation, Elliot Whitter left his console. He avoided the curious glance of his immediate superior and headed directly for Dr. Kelloway. "Might I talk to you for a moment, sir?"

Kelloway adjusted his glasses. "Certainly, Elliot. Got a problem?"

"There's something, sir, I can't figure out."

"You're one of our brightest boys. If you can't figure it out, it must really be a problem."

"Now, I don't really know for certain what's wrong," said Whitter. "It's something, though, in the read-out. I spoke to Dr. Bergen about it a long time back. He said it was the console. But . . . well, could you take a look at it?"

Kelloway made no move to take the young man up on his invitation. "What console are you on?"

"Telemetry. It's 36."

"Oh, sure, Dr. Bergen talked to me about that one. It's supposed to have been fixed, Elliot."

"Maybe so, sir, but I keep getting the same cock-eyed read-outs."

"What exactly?"

72

"See, I did a program on my own, sir, just to check something. That read-out is different."

"You did your own program?"

"See, I don't think it's the console. I think that, somehow, the transmission from Mars isn't—"

"Tell you what, Elliot. We'd better really take that console of yours apart," said Kelloway, briefly putting an arm around the young man's shoulders. "Keep up the good work. With your kind of dedication, you'll be running this whole place someday."

"Well . . . thanks." Whitter, frowning, turned away and walked slowly back to his console.

CHAPTER 13

THE BAR was full of shadows and patches of light, dark wood and Tiffany glass. Under the golden glow of a hanging lamp Bob Caulfield considered the pool table with a leisurely sort of concentration. Cue in hand, he circled the table until he reached the place where his glass of scotch was balanced over a corner pocket. He paused, took a nip, and glanced around the room.

Spotting someone who'd just entered, Caulfield waved and made a come-on-over gesture. "If there's one thing worse than solitary drinking, it's solitary pool-shooting," he said. "So join me in both, Elliot."

Elliot Whitter moved over to the table. "I don't much feel like playing, Bob."

"Oh, so? I've been seriously considering allowing you a chance to win back the fifty smackers you lost when last we met here in the convivial atmosphere of Danny's."

Whitter shook his head. "Naw, I'm not much in the mood."

"Eight ball, five bucks a game?"

"Nope."

"Ten dollars a game."

"Really, I'm serious."

"So am I," said Caulfield, returning to his drink. "I'm dying of a broken heart at the moment, and what would pull me back from the brink of suicide —or worse—is a friendly little game of pool."

"Are you drunk?"

Caulfield considered. "That's a possibility, Elliot. In fact, it could explain why I feel better than I ought to."

"Maybe I need a drink." Whitter turned and made his way to the bar.

Caulfield proceeded to rack up the balls, chalk his cue, and nearly finish his drink.

Whitter came back with a double scotch. He got out of his sport coat and hung it on a nearby rack. "Okay, we'll play."

"Splendid." Caulfield placed the cue ball, then leaned to make a shot.

"How come I never get to break?"

"No reason." With a bow, Caulfield stood aside. "Have at it."

Setting his drink aside and selecting a cue, Whitter approached the table. After more than a minute of scrutiny, he executed a terrible shot, muttered, and stepped back.

Caulfield shook his head. "You usually aren't this lousy," he said. "Have a hard day at the space works?"

Whitter found his drink, gulped at it. "I don't know if I want to talk about it."

"Look, just because I'm one of NBC's best-loved news persons, don't feel you can't confide in me. Actually, I was originally planning to be a priest, and if puberty hadn't caught me unawares, I might be wearing the—"

"This is serious, Bob."

"So was puberty. Boy, that first summer I—"

"The thing is, I don't really know what's going on," said Whitter, leaning on his cue. "See, the numbers come up screwy. So I ran a double check, and then I told Dr. Bergen. He acted . . . you know, he seemed pissed off that I'd found out what I did. He said it was only the console malfunctioning."

"Was he right?"

Whitter frowned. "Well, maybe. He must know what he's doing," he said slowly, not sounding at all convinced. "Anyway, those numbers couldn't have been right."

Ticking his empty glass against his chin, Caulfield asked, "If it's just a stupid mechanical malfunction, why the hell are you so turned around by it?"

"Partly because of the way Bergen reacted. He sort of acted like I was a dumb kid getting a free tour of the place. Humored me, almost patted me on the head."

"Tell me some more about these cockeyed numbers, in clear and concise layman's language."

"What makes it ridiculous," said Whitter, "is that the signals couldn't have come from 300 miles away. Right?"

"Wait a minute. What signals, my boy?"

"The television transmissions," explained Whitter. "They don't seem to be coming from the spacecraft or from Mars. They seem to be coming from Earth."

"Are you trying to con me?"

"I'm trying to tell you what's bothering me. I'm not exactly sure what it means. See, if—"

"Hey, Caulfield! You got a call," the hefty bartender called across the crowded room.

Caulfield put both hands on Whitter's shoulders. "Stay right here, Elliot. I want to hear all the details of this thing." He trotted away, making his way across the room and up to the bar. "A lady?"

"Don't think so." The bartender passed the phone to him.

"Hello, this is Caulfield."

". . . accident over . . . flames . . ."

"Hey, I'm sorry. You'll have to speak louder, we have a rotten connection. Who is this?"

". . . ought to get the story . . ." said the quavering, distant voice. "Right up your . . ."

"I'm not getting this. Speak up, will you?"

". . . get over . . . news . . ."

"Tell you what," said Caulfield, his voice raised, "you call somebody at my assignment desk. If it's something they want me to cover, they'll let me know. And take some diction lessons." He hung up. "Geeze!"

"No romance?"

"Don't think so. As long as I'm so close," he said, "fix me another scotch." While the bartender did that, Caulfield drummed his fingers on the bar.

With his fresh drink, he returned to the pool table.

Whitter was not there. His cue was back in the rack, his coat was gone. There wasn't even a sign of the glass he'd been drinking from.

"Elliot?" Caulfield scanned the area. There was no sign of the young man. "He wouldn't have put on his coat to go to the john."

Sighing, Caulfield began his new drink. Maybe Whitter would come back from wherever it was he'd gone so suddenly.

But he didn't.

CHAPTER 14

WILLIS ROCKED once in his flight couch.

Walker scratched his chin.

Brubaker sat staring straight ahead, at nothing.

"Anybody hungry?" inquired Willis.

"No," said Walker.

"Because if anybody is," continued Willis, "even though we are millions of miles from Earth, I'd be happy to send out for pizza."

Silence again filled the mock Command Module.

Then the hatch opened and a crew-cut, dark-suited young man peered in. "Colonel Brubaker, would the crew like something to eat?"

Brubaker didn't reply.

Finally, Walker said, "We don't need anything."

"Colonel," persisted the crew-cut young man, "Dr. Kelloway wanted to know if you were all comfortable, if your rooms were suitable. I informed him you didn't seem to want to use your rooms, that you haven't left this module much." He coughed carefully into his hand. "Dr. Kelloway thinks perhaps you'd all be a lot more comfortable if you slept in your rooms."

Only silence.

"Colonel Brubaker," the young man said, "how do you feel about that?"

"We prefer to stay here," said Brubaker, not looking at him.

"Well, if there's nothing I can do for you . . . excuse me." He backed out and shut the hatch.

"Now how do you suppose he did that?" said Willis. "Open a hatch from the outside, way out here in the middle of space."

"We are not alone," said Walker.

"You mean there's intelligent life out here in space?"

"Intelligent? I wouldn't exactly say—"

"I'm not going to do it," said Brubaker suddenly.

"Do what?"

"Tomorrow. I am not going to sit here and talk to my wife and tell her how damned fine everything is going," Brubaker amplified. "I can't do it."

"Seems like you've got to," said Walker.

"I have two little kids, with big bright eyes. I used to tell them their dad was going to make them proud of him, as proud as he was of them," said Brubaker, staring straight ahead. "Now I'm supposed to go home and kiss them and look in their eyes. Go home and pretend we really went someplace. Shit, I don't know how I can ever lie like that to them."

"It's not a simple thing, Bru," said Willis.

"We've been sitting around here for three months with our thumbs up our asses," said Brubaker. "Well, I ain't going to do it any more."

"Okay, okay," said Walker, holding up one hand. "Suppose we blow the whistle on this whole scam. We go on nationwide TV tomorrow and tell the truth. What have we accomplished?"

"We'll screw up a lot of people's dinners," suggested Willis.

"We've screwed ourselves already."

"Yeah, but what do we accomplish by screwing everybody else?" asked Walker.

"Now you're starting to sound like Kelloway," Brubaker told him.

"Thanks a lot, buddy."

"You were sounding a shade like him yourself, Bru," said Willis. "Dragging in your bright-eyed kids, and all. I was waiting for you to pull out your tiny violin. Shit, man, we went along with this crazy thing because of you. Now you say you've changed your mind and got religion. If you pull the plug on this, then we are for sure going to be the first ones to go down the drain. No, worse. Our families are going to go first. Man, they'll kill them."

"We are dealing with dudes who put bombs in planes," said Walker. "I don't want that happening to my wife. I told a lot of lies so far; a few more ain't going to matter."

"Okay, okay," said Brubaker. "I know, I know."

In a soundproof booth in a far corner of the sound stage, the young man in the dark suit sat, his eyes on an overhead speaker.

"The thing is," came Brubaker's voice, "I just don't think I can do it tomorrow."

"Wait a minute," Willis said. "All of a sudden I get the feeling you're on a different side than us."

"No, that's not what I'm getting at. I'm trying to say that I may have reached . . . I don't know, a point where I can't keep it up."

"We have to keep it up," insisted Walker. "Kelloway's a madman, and he's probably the sanest one of the bunch that's behind this. We've got families

83

out there, and we're in way too deep to pull out now."

The crew-cut young man reached for the phone and quickly dialed a number.

"But you spend your whole life trying to do something," Brubaker was saying. "And what does it come to? This. What a crock of shit."

"Agreed, it's a crock," said Willis. "But, Bru, it's our crock. We made it, we agreed to wallow in it. And I really think we have to stay in it all the way."

"Don't know if I can."

"Get me Dr. Kelloway," the young man said into the phone. "Dr. Kelloway? I think we may have a problem with Brubaker, come tomorrow."

CHAPTER 15

CAULFIELD slouched. From his seat in the press section of the glass-walled room he could see most of the vast Mission Control room. He scanned the rows of consoles. It was easy to spot Whitter's, because no one was attending it. There was a cover over the screen.

"Keep sitting like that and you're going to grow up with a funny-looking spine," Judy Drinkwater said as she passed in front of him enroute to her seat.

Caulfield reached out and tickled the back side of her knee.

Very covertly she stepped on his toes before moving along.

"Excellent reflexes." Caulfield slipped a Pentel pen out of his inner jacket pocket. After a final glance at Judy he began to look around the room. Reporters to the right of him, reporters to the left. Down in front, the more important types—politicians and the three wives of the astronauts.

Nibbling on the cap of his pen, Caulfield looked again toward the console where Elliot Whitter should have been sitting.

"This is Paul Cunningham, Capricorn Control. We are awaiting the start of the final television transmission from the Command Module on its return to Earth. This transmission is to be a conversation between the crew and their wives. This is the first time the crew has been close enough to Earth to make normal conversation possible."

Bars of color crossed the large wall screen.

"Capricorn One, this is Houston. Capricorn One, this is Houston."

"Houston," came the voice of Brubaker, "this is Capricorn One."

Snow filled the screen. Then a picture of the crew seated in the Command Module popped up.

"Houston, do you have a picture?"

"Roger, Capricorn. We have a picture. There are three very anxious ladies here who'd like to talk to you."

"And we'd like to talk to them," said Walker, grinning.

The women had been provided with microphones. "Jack, it's me."

"Hello there, Betty."

"You look fine."

"Thanks. I can't see you, you know, but you sure sound terrific."

"I miss you, Jack. Very much, and so do the children."

"How are they, the kids?"

"Oh, they're fine. They just miss you."

"Yeah, I know. It's been tough being . . . yeah, tell them I've been missing them a lot, too."

It was Janet Willis' turn next. "Peter, hi."

"I told you never to call me here."

"Are you feeling okay? I guess you are, if you can joke."

"Who's joking? But, seriously, I feel great. How's Sandy?"

"Very well. She got the part of Wendy in her school play. It's *Peter Pan*."

"Acting runs in the family."

Janet said, "You sound so close. It's hard to believe you're really that far away in space."

"It's hard for me to believe, too."

Kay's first words were, "Bru, you look sort of glum."

"Sorry about that. Hi, Kay."

"We're all so very proud of you."

Brubaker winced, and didn't reply immediately.

"Bru, can you still hear me?"

"Sure."

"Hey, Janet," cut in Willis. "Who's playing Captain Hook?"

"Andy Frawley."

"It figures."

"Bru?"

"Yes, Kay."

"I love you."

"I love you," said Brubaker.

"Jack," said Walker's wife, "I meant to tell you, your parents called. They want you to know they're thinking about you all the time."

"That's good, I've been thinking a lot about them."

"Bru, I have a surprise for you," said Kay, reaching into her purse.

"What is it?"

"Charles wrote a composition in school. It won a prize. I want to read it to you."

Brubaker's eyes closed.

"Bru, can't you hear me?"

"Yes, I can hear. Read it, I'd like that."

Kay unfolded the wrinkled sheet of ruled paper. "*My Father* by Charles Brubaker, Jr. That's the title. 'My father is far away from me now. He is flying to Mars. I miss him very much. I always miss him when he goes away. I'm not sad, though. I used to be sad when he went away. One day he told me something. He said that people can't live only for themselves. He said he was trying to do something that would be good for everybody. I know that's what he's doing now. He's doing something for everybody—for me, too. So even though he's far away, he's thinking about me and I'm sort of with him. That's why I'm not sad. That's why I'm so proud.' "

Willis coughed, his eyes on Brubaker. Walker had lowered his head.

Brubaker tried to talk, but he had to clear his throat first.

"Kay, I want to tell you something . . ."

"Bru? What is it?"

Brubaker sat silent for several long seconds. "I want you to know . . . that I love you all. Tell Charlie the composition is just great," he said. "Oh, and tell him that when I get back, I'm going to take him to Yosemite again. Same as last summer."

Kay frowned, then leaned forward with her head shaking slightly from side to side.

Caulfield noticed that. He uncapped his pen and doodled a question mark in his notebook.

"Yes," said Kay, "I will, Bru."

"Time's up, gentlemen."

"Roger, Houston," acknowledged Brubaker.

"The next time we'll be seeing you, you'll be on your way home."

"Amen," said Kay.

Caulfield shut the notebook and went back to chewing on the pen.

CHAPTER 16

CAULFIELD PARKED his four-year-old Mustang casually at the curb and climbed out. He went striding toward the apartment complex. He sprinted up the outside stairs and along the second floor ramp, stopping at a door marked 2A. He knocked. Shifted from foot to foot. Knocked again.

The door opened a few inches and a young, dark-haired woman looked out at him. "Yes?"

"Is Whitter in? Tell him it's Caulfield."

"What?"

"Whitter, Elliot Whitter."

The girl's brow wrinkled and her head ticked from side to side. "There's nobody here by that name," she said. "You have the wrong apartment."

Caulfield took a step back and studied the brass numbers on the door. "Yeah, but this is 2A."

"It is, yes. But these buildings all sort of look alike, you know."

"Yeah, they do. This is 1284 Claridge, isn't it?"

"Well, yes . . ."

"Okay, then Elliot Whitter lives here, at 1284 Claridge, Apartment 2A."

The girl frowned at him. "Is this a joke or what?"

"Elliot is a friend of mine. I've been over here dozens of times. He lives in this apartment."

"He doesn't," insisted the girl. "I do." She began to shut the door.

Caulfield wedged his foot in it, brush salesman style. "Hold on now. I'm not a crazy person and I'm not a mugger. I'm looking for my friend, and he lives here. Really."

"Get your foot out of the doorway," the angry girl ordered, "or I'll call the police."

"Look, I haven't been able to get ahold of him for a while. In fact, the phone company says his number's been disconnected," said Caulfield, keeping his foot in place. "Maybe he moved. How long have you been living here?"

"Two years. Now will you—"

"But that's impossible," said Caulfield. "I know

Elliot was still living in this dump a few months ago. I can prove I've been in this apartment before. I'll describe it for you. It has two rooms, a living room with a dining area and a bedroom."

"So do a hundred other apartments in this complex."

"Okay, but in Elliot's there's modern furniture. There's a brown leather couch and a glass coffee table. And beige carpeting, or possibly tan. Some light brownish color anyway."

The girl stepped back and let the door swing open. "You take a look, and then get the hell out of here."

Caulfield crossed the threshold. He stopped a few steps into the room. There was no carpeting, beige or otherwise. The floors were a dark parquet. The furniture was antique, the couch covered in a flowered print. On the pine coffee table was a sprawl of magazines. He walked over to them, picked one up. It had a subscription tag on it, with the name Sharon Leacock and the apartment address. And the magazine was five weeks old.

"Okay," said the girl, "whatever game you're playing, it's over. You get out now or I will call the cops."

He dropped the magazine to the table. "You honestly don't know Elliot?"

"I never heard of him," she said. "And if he's anything like you, I'm damn glad of that."

"Very curious," said Caulfield. He went to the door. "Nice meeting you." He stepped outside, and she slammed the door at his back.

Caulfield sat in his car for a moment, gazing at the apartment building. With a scowl on his face, he started the engine and pulled away.

It was a hot afternoon, and the highway into Houston shimmered. There wasn't much traffic.

I've known old reporters who pickled their brains with booze, Caulfield said to himself. But I don't think I'm quite at that stage yet. Elliot did live there and now he's vanished. Nobody, though, can vanish without a trace. Going to have to do some . . .

He realized that the Mustang was accelerating rapidly, even though his foot was only resting lightly on the gas pedal. It zoomed from 55 to 60 to 65 to 70 miles an hour.

Caulfield lifted his foot from the gas entirely.

The speed increased to 75.

Concentrating on weaving around the slower cars on the highway, he slammed his foot onto the brake pedal.

The speed increased to 80.

"Holy Jesus!" he remarked, pumping the brake frantically.

The brakes didn't work.

The speed increased to 85.

He was roaring along the highway now, zig-zagging in and out of traffic, darting from lane to lane, to avoid smashing into another vehicle.

Sweat dotted his face and hands.

The speed increased to 90.

Wind seemed to be roaring in his ears. Behind him other drivers were honking their horns.

The Mustang was shivering. The tires were smoking, sending an acrid smell into the car.

Keeping one hand gripped on the wheel, Caulfield yanked the emergency brake.

The speed increased to 95.

Caulfield turned the ignition switch off and jerked the key out. It had no effect on the careening automobile.

"Shit, oh dear," he muttered.

Slam!

He sideswiped another car as he went whizzing by. The Mustang fishtailed, and slid into another lane.

Brakes squealed. Horns barked at him.

He got his car under control, but was shooting along at nearly 100 miles an hour now.

He tried shifting gears, throwing the switch into park, reverse, neutral. Nothing worked.

The speed increased to 110.

Caulfield felt as though he were the car, in some kind of pinball game, roaring at the cars ahead, passing them in a flash, nearly smashing into them. He began pounding on the horn, then decided to keep one hand pressed on it.

The horn sounded like a long, low scream. Or possibly that was him.

There was no way to stop what was happening. The car screamed along the gleaming highway.

The speed increased to 120.

The other cars barely had time to dodge him.

Caulfield noticed something. The highway started to parallel the bayou area. He sucked in a deep breath and gave the steering wheel a very careful, small turn.

The Mustang nearly took flight. It shot across lanes and dug two smoking ruts across the grass of the safety island. For an instant he was rushing in front of traffic coming from the opposite direction.

Then the car left the road. It chopped across a weedy patch of ground and sailed through the air before it nosed down and smacked into the muddy brown water.

Water poured into the open windows.

Caulfield wrestled with the seat belt and got it off. Keep calm, don't panic, his brain advised him. But he felt like opening his mouth and howling.

He couldn't get the car door open.

He felt something enormous pressing at his chest, as though some great creature were hugging him, trying to force him to let out the pitifully small amount of air he had left in his lungs.

Keep calm, don't panic, he thought.

He twisted, shoved, and got himself halfway out of the car, through the open window. He flapped his arms against the murky water and began to rise. Suddenly, though, he was yanked back.

His pants' leg was caught on something—the door handle, perhaps.

An impulse was growing—an impulse to let out the air that was burning in his lungs, sending needles of pain through his body.

He tugged and spun in the water.

Then, he wasn't sure why, he was rising again, his leg free of the car.

It took forever, it seemed, forever and a little more to get to the surface. He climbed and climbed, his feet kicking, his arms churning at the water.

Finally there was sunlight, and then muddy brown. Finally there was air to breathe. He let out his breath and then gulped in air. It was like drinking a quart of gin all at once. He felt woozy, like doubling up.

He didn't. He made himself swim, and in a few moments he was back on the weedy shore. He got as far as the ruts his dead and gone Mustang had plowed in the earth. Dropping to his knees, he rested.

Cars had stopped on the highway above. People were making their way down to him.

Caulfield realized that it had probably only been a minute or so ago that he had shot off the road. It didn't feel like that.

"Are you okay?" asked the perspiring black man who reached him first. "What the hell happened?"

"That," said Caulfield in a very dim voice, "is one very good question."

CHAPTER 17

WHILE THE astronauts dressed, a voice from an overhead speaker told them what they were supposed to be doing.

"This is Paul Cunningham, Capricorn Control. We are 259 days, 14 hours, 12 minutes into the flight. All systems are nominal. The prime recovery ship, the U.S.S. *Oriskany,* is in position. The flight director advises that the prime recovery helicopter is tail number 2665, the secondary recovery helicopter is tail number 2664. An on-target landing should result in a recovery time of 18 minutes from splashdown to the opening of the hatch. After the crew delivers its speech on the deck of the *Oriskany* and is welcomed aboard by Captain Franklin Thorne, they will be taken below decks for a medical debriefing. Tonight at 1800 hours Pacific Daylight Time, the crew will attend a victory banquet, topped off by a special dessert—a forty-foot-high red cake depicting the Martian surface."

"Yum, yum," said Willis. "That makes it all worthwhile. These months of bullshit won't seem so bad when I get that special dessert."

"Aw, we won't get to eat it," said Walker. "Kelloway probably got a way to fake that, too."

"Don't be such a pessimist, Jack."

From out of the overhead speaker came more voices.

"Capricorn One, this is Houston."

"Roger, Houston."

"You are go for CSM-CM separation."

"Roger, Houston."

Head tilted, Willis glanced up at the speaker. "You've got a terrific voice, Bru. Have you ever thought of going into radio?"

Brubaker gave him a sour look.

"You'd make a nifty disc jockey," suggested Walker.

"You are 17 minutes, 44 seconds from Entry Interface."

"We copy."

"We are reading ECS of 1424."

"1424 ECS."

"Guidance should be set for Spica and Numa."

"Guidance on Spica and Numa."

The door of the room was pushed open carefully. A crew-cut young man stepped in. "Gentlemen, if you'll come along with me now, please."

"Shit, just when it was getting to the good part," complained Walker.

"I actually think," said Willis, moving for the door, "I like the *Adventures of Colonel Brubaker, Planeteer* better than *As The World Turns.*"

"Oh, so do I," said Walker. "It's much sadder."

"A three-hankie show for sure."

"Gentlemen, please. Your jet is waiting."

They made their way through the sound stage hangar, cutting across the red face of Mars, and stepped into the glaring desert day.

The Falcon jet, door open and engines already whining, was waiting nearby.

Very rapidly they were escorted inside, and the ship took off.

Another crew-cut young man told them, as the jet knifed across the clear blue sky, "We have a chopper waiting for you on the island. It'll take you to the spacecraft when it splashes down."

"Looks like we're going first class," remarked Willis.

The crew-cut man ignored him, addressing himself to Brubaker. "The chopper will transport you

100

to the craft, as I was saying. It will take the *Oriskany* more than an hour and a half to reach you, so there won't be any rush."

"No rush," said Brubaker.

CHAPTER 18

"THRUSTERS, guidance, navigation checklist complete."

"Roger, Capricorn. You are go for CSM-CM separation."

Dr. Kelloway was pacing. He readjusted his glasses and gazed again around the Mission Control room.

One of the technicians at the tracking consoles caught his eye and indicated he needed to talk to him.

Kelloway went over to him. "How does it look, Marschall?"

"Could be we have a slight problem, sir."

"Oh, what?"

Marschall punched a few keys and indicated the blip on the readout screen. "They may be a little off target."

"How far?"

"Might be as much as 200 miles."

Kelloway rubbed at his chin. "200, huh?"

"Which means it may take an hour and a half for the recovery forces to reach them."

"That's an unexpected problem," said Kelloway. "But not a terribly serious one, I don't think. You keep me posted, though."

"I will, sir."

Kay Brubaker picked up her coffee cup, then set it down.

Janet Willis got up, crossed the Brubaker living room, and turned up the sound on the television set.

Betty Walker picked up her coffee cup, then set it down.

"Capricorn, we are 10 seconds from Interface."

"Roger, Houston."

"8, 7, 6, 5, 4 . . ."

"This is the worst part," said Betty quietly, "the worst part of all so far."

". . . 3, 2, 1. Interface."

"Roger, Houston."

The television screen showed them the Mission Control room, and it let them hear an odd buzzing sound—not a comforting sound, a warning sound.

"My God," said Kay, "what is it?"

"Capricorn One, this is Houston. Capricorn One, this is Houston."

No answer. The buzzing went on.

"Capricorn One, we have a red on the heat shield. Do you copy?"

"My God, my God," repeated Kay, pressing a hand between her breasts.

"Capricorn One, this is Houston. We show red. Do you copy?"

A nine-year-old boy came running into the living room. "I was at Kennie's and I'm late, mom. Did I miss—"

"Charlie!" Kay jumped up, moved to the boy. "You'd better . . . you'd better wait outside."

"Capricorn One, this is Houston. Do you read?"

"Why, mom? What's the—"

"Outside. Out of here!" She put an arm around him and almost dragged him across the room toward the doorway.

"Capricorn One, this is Houston. Capricorn One, this is Houston."

CHAPTER 19

"THIS AIN'T no island," observed Walker.

"It does, now you mention it, look strangely like our point of departure," said Willis, as their jet set down on the desert landing field again.

A crew-cut young man came into the cabin from the pilot area. "There's been a change in schedule."

"How can that be?" asked Willis.

"You'll be waiting here a bit longer than anticipated."

"Something went wrong," said Brubaker. "That's it, isn't it?"

The crew-cut young man opened the door. "If you'll return to the hangar," he suggested, "you'll eventually be filled in on all the changes in the overall plan."

"One thing's for sure," said Walker. "We never going to get a piece of that cake."

Caulfield came clomping down the slanting carpeted aisle of the NASA auditorium. "Is this seat taken?"

"Yes," replied Judy Drinkwater. "I'm saving it for a Japanese wrestler of my acquaintance."

"You shouldn't be so whimsical, Judith," advised Caulfield, as he settled in beside the blonde. "This is a very somber occasion."

"Anytime you're within ten feet of me it's a somber occasion."

Flashbulbs began to pop, cameras began to whir. Dr. Kelloway, accompanied by several other NASA officials, had stepped upon the stage.

He took a seat at the center of the table on the stage. When the others were seated, Kelloway took hold of a microphone and cleared his throat, which boomed across the auditorium.

"Well, ladies and gentlemen," he said, his voice

strained. "Um . . . I have a brief statement for you, after which I'll answer your questions."

From a pocket of his coat Kelloway withdrew a folded sheet of white paper. He unfolded it, carefully spread it on the table, and began reading:

"At T-plus 259 days, 15 hours, 11 minutes in the flight of Capricorn One, which was 2 minutes 18 seconds after interface, the heat shield warning light on the Mission Control monitoring panel turned red. We attempted to establish radio contact with the spacecraft, but we were not successful. 14 seconds later, 2 minutes 32 seconds after interface, the tracking monitor lost its signal. Contact was never reestablished."

Kelloway paused to rub a hand across his forehead, then continued: "All the other monitoring data confirmed the loss of the craft. Um . . . the heat shield evidently separated from the Command Module. As you know, the heat shield is the only protection the module has against the heat buildup on reentering the Earth's atmosphere. The spacecraft disintegrated within 12 seconds after the loss of the shield."

He turned the sheet of paper over slowly. "We don't know the cause of the heat shield failure. This has never happened before. I . . . I can't adequately describe how we feel. These men . . . they were an integral part of a family here in the program. I don't have to tell you what kind of personal qualities they possessed. This malfunction was the only one which occurred in the months of the flight. We don't know why it happened. That's the end of my statement."

Judy was on her feet. "Couldn't you have anticipated this sort of malfunction?"

"We try to anticipate everything, Judy," answered Kelloway. "But the possibility that something like this could happen in spite of all our precautions is always there. We have to learn to live with that sort of thing."

Across the room another reporter asked, "When was the last time the heat shield was checked out?"

"All during the reentry phase there was a series of status checks. All of them gave every indication the shield was in place," answered Kelloway. "The system was checked out by the flight crew and by Mission Control."

"What has been the White House reaction to what's happened?"

"I haven't spoken to the President. I'm sure I will fairly soon. I would like to say the President has been a source of constant encouragement to us in the program. This mission meant as much to him as it did to us."

"Do you think this will end the Manned Space Program?"

"I don't know. In 1967 we had an Apollo One fire. Grissom, White and Chafee died. We were all crushed, but we just didn't give up. We went on, as they would have wanted us to," said Kelloway. "Two years later Neil Armstrong walked on the moon."

"But you can't tell us for certain that the program will continue?"

"Today three remarkable men have given their lives," said Kelloway. "They gave their lives for something which meant more to them than their personal survival. I ask you, all of you here . . . and all of the people of this country—you be the ones to give the answer. How can we best serve these men? By giving up on their dream? By saying it was all for nothing? You give me the answer."

CHAPTER 20

BRUBAKER said it first. "We're dead."

They were back in the same windowless room where they had first been brought months ago. Wearing their white jump suits, standing around, wondering, and waiting.

"Huh?" said Walker.

"We're dead."

"Heck, and I was such a terrific guy," said Willis.

Brubaker said, "Figure it out. Something must have happened during reentry, otherwise we'd be winging our way to the splashdown spot right now."

"Guess you're right," said Willis. "Only a couple

of possibilities when you think about it. Either the trajectory was kaflooey and the thing landed hundreds or thousands of miles from target, or it never landed at all."

"Yeah, but even if it landed in Siberia," said Walker, "they'd have told us by now. Explain how they was going to slip us behind the Iron Curtain, or whatever."

"What it looks like," said Brubaker, "is that the damned thing never landed at all. Either the heat shield separated or the chutes never opened."

"So we're dead," said Willis.

"I'll bet you that right now Kelloway is making a speech about what brave and wonderful lads we all were."

"The idea of somebody delivering my eulogy while I'm still above ground," said Willis, "doesn't cheer me up."

"Think about this now," said Brubaker. "If anybody ever sees us again, then all the dominoes will start to fall. It's as simple as that. They can't afford to let that happen."

"Kelloway might come to his senses," said Walker, without much conviction. "Fess up and let us face the music."

"Bullshit," said Brubaker. "Do you see that madman transporting us home to Houston and having a press conference to announce it was all just a good-natured prank?"

"Seems unlikely," said Willis.

"So what avenue does that leave for them? They are going to have to see to it that nobody ever sees us alive."

Walker punched his palm with his fist. "Hold on now, Bru. I heard about situations like this. Well, not exactly like this, but where the FBI or the CIA or somebody wanted to hide a witness or a spy who couldn't ever go home again. So they give the dude a new face and a new ID. They could do that to us, don't you think?"

"And run the risk that someday, maybe even in our sleep, one of us might say something?"

"Also," put in Willis, "I don't think we're dealing with a group that's also going to provide face jobs for our wives and kids. I mean, it would look odd if all our families suddenly vanished." He scratched his head. "Although it might not be bad spending the rest of my life with Robert Redford's face."

"Let's remember," Brubaker said to Walker, "that these guys are the ones who got us in line in the first place by threatening to blow up our families. Buddy, I don't think that was a bluff."

Walker nodded, "No, neither do I."

"Plastic surgery, new IDs—that's too much trouble, when one little chunk of plastic explosive can do the job. Or three or four very inexpensive bullets."

Walker rubbed his hands together. "You figure that jet is still setting out there?"

"Odds are it is."

"Then," suggested Walker, as he eased toward the door, "I'd like to make a motion that we vacate." He took hold of the door handle.

The door was locked.

"If we needed any proof," said Brubaker, "that locked door does it."

"Leave us leave," said Willis. "We ought to be able to smash that frigging door down."

They were.

A crew-cut young man met them in the hall. "I'll have to ask you fellows to—"

"Nope." Walker stepped up to him and decked him with two punches. "Very satisfying."

"Boy, you people are natural boxers," said Willis, as they hurried along the corridor.

"Say goodbye to Mars." Walker was in the lead as they cut across the imitation Martian surface.

Brubaker slid the hangar door open a couple of feet. "Guy watching the plane."

"Let's fake him out," suggested Willis, "by just strolling up to the jet. You know, very casual."

"Might work." Brubaker went first and the other two followed.

A crew-cut young man in a blue suit was standing by a stairway that led into the open cockpit of the Falcon jet. He glanced at them, a slight frown touching his face.

"They tell us we're to get back aboard," said Brubaker, smiling at the young man.

The young man returned the smile. "Are you sure? I haven't been—"

"If we wasn't sure," said Walker, "we wouldn't be here, 'cause we never do nothing without being ordered to first."

"In fact—" said Brubaker. He slammed a fist into the young man's stomach, then brought both hands hard against his neck when the man doubled over.

Swiftly Willis and Walker lugged the unconscious man over against the hangar.

"All aboard," said Brubaker, while dashing up the stairway into the ship.

When the three were in the cockpit and strapped in, Brubaker, in the pilot's seat, got the craft going. The jet's fans began to turn and the plane swung away from the hangar.

"Farewell committee," said Willis, nodding at the hangar.

Three more men came running out of it, waving their hands.

Brubaker guided the jet into a taxi position on the runway.

Two of the men ran back toward the hangar; the third stood on the runway with both arms semaphoring.

"They really must like us," said Walker. "They don't want us to leave."

"That's the way with parties," said Willis. "I always hate to be the first to leave."

Brubaker started the jet along the runway. "They aren't going to give up this easily, so watch out."

"Car," said Willis, looking back over his shoulder.

A heavy black auto had come shooting out of the hangar and was speeding along in their wake.

"Maybe they want to play chicken," said Walker.

The car raced by them and kept going. Then it suddenly swung across the runway and stopped.

Brubaker was tugging back on the stick. "Bastards," he said.

"If we smash that car," said Willis, swallowing, "you know they're going to bill us for it."

"Here we go," said Brubaker.

The jet lifted off the ground and cleared the top of the car by only a few feet.

"Nice going, Smilin' Jack," Walker said to Brubaker.

Willis let out a small sigh. "Hurdle number one taken care of," he said. "You guys got any idea where we are?"

"No," said Brubaker.

"How about where we're going?"

"West," Brubaker answered. "Once we hit the coast we'll go north until we hit a city. All we have to do is get someplace where there are people. A newspaper, a TV station. All we have to do is show up and be seen. Then it's over."

"I don't know if it's exactly over," said Willis.

CHAPTER 21

A SMALL buzzing sound.

"Jesus," said Brubaker, glancing at the cockpit dash. "The fuel, there's no damned fuel."

"I told you, whenever we take a trip," said Willis, "you should always fill the tank."

"What about the reserve?" asked Walker.

"It's on reserve now."

"Terrific," said Walker.

"I'll start to circle," said Brubaker, "find us a flat place to set down."

Willis was staring out the window. "There's a heck of a lot of nothing down there, Bru."

In every direction there was nothing but yellow

sand, spills of jagged rock, and low, reddish cliffs.

"There, over that way," said Walker, "other side of those cliffs. A place, maybe, to land."

"Yeah, looks like we'll have about 4,000 feet. Should be enough." Brubaker extended the landing gear, banked the aircraft sharply, and skimmed over the desert basin. "Everybody strap in. This ain't going to be smooth."

"You sure you know how to land this thing?" Willis inquired, as he used the safety belt.

"Land it? Nope, I only got up to the lesson on how to fly it. Not to worry, though."

All at once they were touching down, the wheels digging into the sand. Yellow clouds rose up, spinning around the jet. The ship bounced, swayed, and came to a stop, its nose down.

After a moment Willis said, "That was fun, daddy. Can we buy some more tickets and do it again?"

Walker unbuckled. "Didn't do the plane much good. Busted up the wing some."

Brubaker was out of his seat, getting the cabin door open. "End of the line, all out."

The three of them wiggled their way out of the ruined jet and dropped to the bright sand. Everything glared—the mountain ridge on their left and the dry, flat desert that extended in every other direction. There was a scattering of scrubby brush, but nothing else. Not a sign of life or water.

"Well, we didn't get to Mars," said Willis, "but this is darned close."

Shielding his eyes, Brubaker was looking skyward. "I figure we got about a twenty-minute lead on them. It's going to be easy to spot this plane from up there," he said. "We've two choices, as I see it: We stay together, or we split up and head out of here in different directions."

Walker kicked at the sand. "Suppose we'll do better if we split up."

"Theoretically," said Brubaker.

"Well, if we go in three different directions," said Walker, "we triple the odds of one of us getting through."

"That's the point," said Brubaker. "But going solo adds to the individual risk. As a team we can meet an emergency better."

Willis shook his head. "Yeah, but we can't afford that luxury, Bru. The important thing is for at least one of us to reach civilization and blow the whistle on this caper."

"Okay, agreed," said Brubaker. "We split up."

"They probably packed a survival kit in this thing." Willis boosted himself back up into the lopsided ship. A moment later he returned with a gray metal box. "Got it." He carefully placed the box at their feet and squatted to open it.

The survival kit contained three cans of water, a flint, and a .38-caliber pistol with twelve rounds

118

of ammunition. There were also four flares, a first aid kit, a transistor signal radio, an inflatable life raft, a mirror, a flashlight, and a box of matches.

"Can I have the raft?" said Willis. "With all this sand, I could use a beach toy."

"Okay, there's a can of water for each of us," Brubaker said, as he doled out the water ration.

"No Pepsi?" said Willis, slipping his can inside his jump suit.

"A flare each." Brubaker handed them out, keeping the extra one for himself. "Jack, you take the flint. Pete and I will split the matches."

"I don't need matches," said Willis, taking them. "I was a boy scout."

"How about the gun?" asked Walker.

Brubaker said, "You want it?"

"Guns make me nervous."

"I always shoot myself in the foot," said Willis.

"I'll take it then," said Brubaker. After he stowed the pistol and the ammunition on himself, he picked up the mirror and snapped it in half. "Half for me, half for you, Jack."

"Don't I get any?" inquired Willis. "I just know my makeup's going to get ruined in this dreadful desert."

Brubaker leaned for a moment against the fuselage of the jet. "Remember, if anybody gets caught, or can't make it, try to set off a flare. That way the others will know," he said. "I'll continue west. Jack, you try south, and Pete, head north. We came from the east, so we know that's the wrong way."

"I saw John Wayne do something like this in a movie once," said Walker.

"Yeah, but he had Sophia Loren along with him," said Willis.

Straightening up, Brubaker said, "There's not much time, so we'll skip the farewell speeches. Let's go." He took a few steps and halted. "I figure we'll all make it, but in case somebody doesn't . . . well . . ."

"Did I ever tell you about the guy who had a job giving enemas to elephants and he—"

"Tell it to me when we get home," Walker interrupted Willis.

After a few more seconds of hesitation, they separated, each heading away from the downed plane alone.

CHAPTER 22

CAULFIELD cut across the midday lawn, dodging the two languid workmen who were clearing away the last evidence that the media had been camping around the Brubaker house. He took the steps two at a time and rang the bell.

The door opened and a uniformed cop looked out at him. "Yeah?"

"I'd like to see Mrs. Brubaker. My name is Caulfield."

"I'm afraid she's not seeing anyone at the moment."

"I phoned this morning," Caulfield told him. "I think she's expecting me."

"What was your name again?"

"Caulfield."

"Okay, wait a sec." The policeman turned away.

Caulfield waited on the porch, hands in his pockets. He whistled, tried out a few tap steps, then slouched.

The policeman returned. "She'll see you," he said. "Come on in."

The house was quiet, shadowy.

"She's out on the patio," explained the cop, pointing. "Through that door there."

"Much obliged." He found Kay Brubaker sitting on a bright, patterned couch on the red-tiled patio, a white-painted arbor with twisting grape leaves shading her from the bright sun. "Hi, Mrs. Brubaker."

"Sit down, Mr. Caulfield," Kay invited.

He settled into a wrought iron chair, tapped his knees, sucked his cheek, and scratched his head. "First off," he began, "it goes without saying that I'm very sorry about . . . and I apologize for barging in at a time like this."

"Don't be too uncomfortable around me, okay?" Kay said. "You are interrupting me, but that's exactly what I want now—something to distract me. And you did mention that what you wanted to talk about was important."

"It may not be important to you," he said. "I'm

not sure. It's important to me, in a sort of personal way."

"I've seen you on the news, now and then," she said. "You're on a story now?"

"Well, in a way. But as I mentioned to you when I called, I'm not looking for an interview." Caulfield shifted, slapped his knees again. "What I want to ask you about is the last time you spoke to your husband. You know, after the landing."

"Yes?"

"This may sound sort of goofy, ma'am," he began, clearing his throat and leaning toward her. "I was there at Mission Control, watching you while you spoke with your husband. Now just before the conversation ended, Colonel Brubaker mentioned something to you about a vacation. You didn't seem to understand what he was talking about. I've just been over at our local station, checking out a video tape of the incident, and my impression checks out right. You look confused."

Kay nodded her head. "You're right," she replied. "But exactly why do you want to know?"

"As I told you, ma'am, right now it's personal."

"Well, it happens to be personal to me, too."

"Listen, I'm not trying to embarrass you or anyone else."

She studied his face. "I remember thinking, when I saw you on the news, Mr. Caulfield, that you weren't exactly like the ordinary newsman," she said. "You're more flippant, for one thing, but there's a sort of honesty about you."

"I'm not just another pretty face, no. And I'm not trying to con you, or get a story out of you."

"It's really sort of silly, nothing at all dramatic or mysterious," Kay said slowly, her eyes nearly closing. "Bru must have forgotten, made a little mistake. I'm sure that's all it was. He obviously had a lot on his mind, and it's natural he might get mixed up about a vacation."

"Mixed up?" Caulfield was leaning forward. "Specifically what was wrong with what he said?"

"What are you looking for?" she asked.

"It has to do with a friend of mine," he told her. "Could be this has nothing to do with it at all. Did you ever work one of those puzzles, when you were a kid—the kind where you shade in the dotted squares? At first it doesn't look like anything. But when you get enough squares filled in, all of a sudden you have a picture."

"Charlie loved to do those, a year or so ago," said Kay. "You think your friend's problem, and something Bru made a mistake about, are linked somehow?"

"I've only filled in a few squares, ma'am, not enough yet to tell," he said. "Believe me, when I get a picture, and if it's the picture I'm expecting, I'll tell you the whole thing."

Kay said, "What Bru went wrong on was the

vacation. He said we'd go back to Yosemite, like last year. But last year we didn't go to Yosemite, we went to Flat Rock, in Arizona." She made a small shrug. "That's all. It doesn't seem to be of cosmic significance, does it?"

Caulfield squeezed his nose, poking his cheek out with his tongue. "It might, it just might." He stretched up out of the chair. "It's very pleasant out here."

"It used to be." Kay stood, too, and walked toward the door with him.

"Anyway, I appreciate your listening to my somewhat nitwit questions."

"Have I been of any help?"

"I've got a hunch you have, but don't ask me how, yet." Caulfield reached out, took hold of her hand, and shook it. "I'd like to call you again, if I come up with anything. May I?"

"Yes, of course."

"Thanks, then." He tried out a grin, let it fade, and went away from her.

CHAPTER 23

THE SOUND of the helicopters grew louder and louder.

Brubaker did not move. "Goddamn ostrich," he murmured, "is what I feel like."

The two choppers must have been almost directly over him, because their roaring was loud as hell. They dangled there, a few hundred feet above him.

He was stretched out in a crevice, in a jagged ditch between two low ridges of rocky ground, and blanketed with hastily applied sand, scarcely breathing.

126

Do they see me? he wondered.

They were staying above him, hanging in the glaring sky. Watching, waiting.

Wonder what Kelloway told them to do? Shoot me soon as they spot me? Or take me alive?

Could be it wasn't even Kelloway's decision to make anymore. There were others involved, other madmen. No telling what kind of ruthless choices they were capable of.

Did the copters sound further off? Were they going away?

Brubaker remained flat out, listening. Could be a trick. Go away, and then come back.

The chuffing sound of the rotating blades was definitely getting fainter.

More minutes melted away. There was only silence in the sky.

Brubaker kept waiting, not moving. After another five long, hot minutes he allowed himself to sit up, sand falling away from him.

Far off, darting toward the shimmering horizon, were two dots which must be the copters.

"They didn't see me, I got under cover in time," he said, relieved. He stood, brushing the yellow grit from his clothes, running his dry tongue over his cracked lips. Sand had gotten into the stubble on his face, and he had to rub it out with his blistered, cut hands.

"So, I've got some more time," he said, as he

started moving westward again. "How much, though? How much?"

☐ ☐ ☐

"This is not exactly," Caulfield said to himself, "the garden spot of the universe."

He parked his rented car at what passed for a curb in the small, collapsing town he had just entered. Flat Rock, Arizona, covered about two blocks and looked like the set for a very low-budget movie Western. The wooden buildings leaned against each other like weary old men, the sidewalks were swayback stretches of ruined planking.

In his shirt sleeves, with the shirt sticking to him, Caulfield slid out of the car and stood in the dusty yellow street. He wiped at his perspiring forehead, then squinted. On a lopsided pole to his right hung a weathered sign. " 'Welcome to Flat Rock, Arizona,' " he read aloud. " 'Authentic Frontier Town. Flat Rock was first settled in 1858 and abandoned in 1889. It remains intact and is preserved and protected by the Department of the Interior.' " Caulfield blew his breath over his lips. "You Interior boys aren't doing such a hot job."

Flat Rock had obviously died twice. In the window of the ancient general store across the street were decals for BankAmericard and American Express. But the door of the place was boarded over and, except for some kind of chubby lizard sunning on a dry plank, there was no life in Flat Rock.

Caulfield crossed to the defunct general store. He brushed his sweating chest. "Am I getting too old for leg work?" There was an authentic looking hitching post in front of the store. Caulfield leaned his buttocks against it, scanned the dusty street.

Crash!

Window glass was exploding all around him.

Hit the dirt! he advised himself, doing just that. He dived and landed belly-down in the street.

The hitching post made a very strange noise and splintered, sending sharp slivers flying.

Caulfield rolled, hugging himself along the street and into a dark alley between the old store and what was left of a livery stable. The third bullet from the high-powered rifle ate into the spot where he'd been a few seconds earlier.

Panting, perspiring like a fiend, Caulfield crouched in the shadows and waited. He quickly inspected the ground around him, but saw nothing he could use as a weapon—not even a big rock. "Hand-to-hand combat isn't my strong suit," he reflected, "especially against some son of a bitch with a rifle."

Nothing happened.

Then he heard a car engine grind to life. At a

distance, at the other end of this dead town, a car went growling away.

Very cautiously, Caulfield edged out into the hot, yellow street.

A car, some kind of green station wagon, was barreling the hell out of Flat Rock, sending spiraling clouds of murky dust into the air.

"I think I'm going to have to apply for hazard pay, if this keeps up." Walking, still a shade gingerly, he hurried back to his own car.

CHAPTER 24

KELLOWAY'S HAND held the car phone tightly. "Three men on foot," he was saying into the mouthpiece. "How far can they have gotten? You've got to keep looking until you find them." He hung up, slid out of his auto, and saw the boy watching him from the lawn.

"Hi, Uncle Jim," called Charlie Brubaker.

"Hi, Charles." He forced himself to grin. "Your mom around?"

"Out back, on the patio." The boy ran up to him and took his hand. "Come on, I'll show you."

Kay was sitting quietly in a wicker chair, an untouched glass of iced tea on the wrought iron table beside her. "Hello, Jim."

"You're looking fine," he said, sitting near her.

"All things considered. Can I offer you anything?"

"Nothing, thanks." He shook his head. "Everybody doing all right?"

She turned to her son. "You go play, Charlie."

"Aw, I wanted to talk to Uncle Jim."

"I'll drop in and chat before I go," Kelloway promised.

"Okay," said the boy forlornly, as he shuffled away reluctantly.

"Did you have something more to talk about?" Kay asked, when the boy was gone.

"Well, Kay," began Kelloway, "there's going to be a memorial service on Tuesday, here in Houston, at the Veterans Cemetery. The President will be coming, to make a speech."

"Very nice. Will I get a folded flag to keep among my souvenirs?"

Kelloway watched the shadowy patterns on the patio stones. "I'd like you to be there."

"I really don't see the purpose."

"I know how tough everything is right now," said Kelloway. "It's just that it would be good for everyone if you'd come to this service with me."

Kay shuddered suddenly. "A horrible way to die, it was a horrible way to die."

"No, not really, Kay. When the heat shield separated . . . it was over in less than five seconds."

"Oh? And would you like to go through five seconds like that?"

"Okay, I know how grizzly I'm sounding. But, Kay, what I'm trying to get across is that Bru never suffered," Kelloway told her. "And he died doing what he wanted to do, something he felt was important enough to die for."

"I know what he felt," said Kay. "I guess I simply don't agree it was all that important."

"I can understand that." Very slowly he got out of his chair. "I'm sorry to intrude on you like this, Kay. I'll talk to you tomorrow."

"Jim," she said. "I'll go."

"Thank you," he said. "You're a very special woman."

"He was a very special man."

"He was that." Kelloway turned his back on her and walked away.

Charlie was sitting on the front lawn, poking at the grass with a twig. "Uncle Jim . . ." he said.

Kelloway crossed over and squatted beside him. "Yes, Charlie?"

"Can you tell me about my dad?"

"Well, Charlie, it's—"

"I mean about how he went to Mars," said the boy. "About what it was like there."

Kelloway put an arm around the boy's narrow shoulders. "Yes, sure, I can tell you about that."

CHAPTER 25

RED.

The sky, the burning ground, the jagged rocks. Everything was a glaring, hazy red.

Walker rubbed at his eyes. He stumbled, fell to his knees. The hot, gritty earth tore at his skin, rasping at the spots already raw and bloody.

"Dehydrating," he muttered through cracked lips. "Dehydrating."

He pushed at the ground with his battered black hands, and managed to rise once more.

His jump suit was tattered. He felt as though he were made of sand—dry, blazing sand. After a few shallow breaths, which seemed to bring no air inside him at all, Walker resumed his shambling progress.

"Look for signs," he said in a quaking voice. "Look for signs, like the manual says, of water . . ."

He fell down again.

Must have passed out for awhile. When he got to his feet, there was a different feel and look to things. The day felt older, the glaring light a little less intense.

Walker stood there, palms pressed against his thighs, swaying. "Got to go by the book," he told himself. "Look for signs . . . signs of water . . ."

He shambled on—swaying, stumbling, falling, rising.

It went on and on.

He lost his footing on the crushed edge of a dried-up river bed. Down he rolled, coming to rest in its sandy bottom.

"Lowest part of . . . dried river bed," he recited. "Lowest part . . . outside . . . of bend . . . look for . . . bend . . ."

He made his way on hands and knees, ripping away the fresh scabs.

"Lowest part of . . . the bend . . ."

Walker found what he thought must be the right place to dig for water. With unsteady hands, he dug into his shredded jump suit. "Where . . . is . . . where is that . . . damn . . ." His fingers located the half-mirror. He pulled it out.

The sun caught it and made it flare with light,

as Walker started to dig, with a weary frenzy, at the gritty river bed.

"Going to find . . . find water . . . like the manual . . . manual promised . . . not going to . . . to dry up . . . blow away . . . shit . . . not going to do that . . ."

Sand. Nothing but sand. And after that, more sand.

He kept digging, until there was no strength left in him.

Fighting against it, Walker sank down. "Not going to give up . . . Liz, I know . . . water's here . . . it is . . . can't give you up, Liz . . . if there was just only a . . . little bit . . . little bit of water . . . that's all I . . ."

He sprawled out, his hand clutching the chunk of mirror. The sun touched it once more, making light glint off it.

Maybe he lost a little more time. He wasn't sure. He felt rested. Yeah, he could keep digging. Find that water and then he'd be okay.

Something made him look up.

Two birds were way the hell up there, circling him. That was okay. Birds always circled over water. The manual told you that.

"Unless they're . . ." What was the name of those birds that came and ate you after you were dead. "They call 'em . . . shit . . . I know it . . ."

He kept staring up into the glare of the afternoon sky, watching the birds grow larger and larger and hearing their steady chuffing sound.

"Vultures," he remembered.

Only they weren't vultures. They weren't birds at all.

The sand began to swirl and spin, rushing at him in gritty clouds.

"Choppers," he said, realizing they'd found him and the game was over.

Yesterday he would have gotten up and run from them, made them work to capture him.

That was yesterday.

Today he stayed where he was, caring about only one thing—hoping that maybe they'd let him have just a little bit of water.

Kelloway was back in his chilly air-conditioned office. He leaned back in his chair, studying the framed photos on the walls—especially those which showed him and Brubaker together, arm in arm, side by side, smiling.

"The good old days," he murmured. The phone rang. "Yes?"

"They've found one of them," came a crisp voice.

"Which one? Was it Bru—"

"Walker."

"He was alone?"

"All alone. Apparently they split up."

"Which direction was he heading from the jet?"

"North."

"Then all you have to do is look south and west from now on. Call off the other searchers and concentrate on south and west."

"Yes, we'd already decided on that." The phone was hung up.

Kelloway hung up on his end. He glanced again at the wall photos. "I hope you're alive when they find you, Bru," he said softly.

CHAPTER 26

"I'M here again."

"So I noticed. Come in."

Caulfield stepped out of the afternoon, into the Brubaker house, and followed Kay along a hallway.

"Would you like something to drink?" she asked, stopping beside the small built-in bar in the living room.

"I would indeed."

"Scotch?"

"With a little ice."

She fixed two drinks, and handed him one. "You haven't found what you're looking for," she said.

"You feel embarrassed about bothering me again. But there are just one or two more questions you'd like to ask. It's something personal, and then you won't bother me anymore."

"Very neat," he said, smiling at her. "When I was a kid there was a guy on television who could read minds like that. Dunninger was his name." He drank some of his drink.

Kay, watching him, seated herself in an armchair. "You're up to something, Mr. Caulfield," she said. "You want my help, but you won't tell me. Why?"

"You're a very astute person."

"I am, but you're avoiding an answer."

Slumping onto a sofa, he said, "Okay, I'm a guy who drinks more than he should at times, and gets into more trouble than he should. I tend to see things not quite like most other people do. Maybe there's a different drummer somewhere in my background. Anyway, I have a hunch. Right now I'm working on a lalapalooza of a hunch. Something wrong is going on, and I think I'm starting to see what it is."

Kay said, "What exactly are you after?"

"Something damn important," he told her. "I'm sure it is, because they keep trying to kill me."

"What?"

He held up a hand. "Didn't mean to bring that up," Caulfield said hurriedly. "Only people who suspect they're being plotted against are goofy. But two times lately seems more than a coincidence."

"I don't see what—"

"Trust me awhile, on the rest of the details, ma'am. But please don't think I'm goofy."

"You're not goofy. But you are exasperatingly mysterious."

"I think maybe I'm taking a hell of a risk telling you any of this," he said, after taking in some more scotch. "The thing is, I don't believe your husband is the kind of man who makes mistakes. No matter how far away he is. I think he wanted to tell you something."

Kay was leaning forward now. "You keep talking about Bru in the present tense, as though you think he is still alive." She hesitated. "Do you?"

Caulfield avoided her eyes. "Trust me a little longer, huh? Let me ask you the questions."

Gradually she leaned back in the chair again. "All right. You think Bru was trying to tell me something when he made that mistake about the vacations."

"It wasn't a mistake," said Caulfield. "Now what did you do at Flat Rock?"

"Nothing much really," she answered. "We were only there a day because Charlie came down with something."

"Okay, but what did you do that one day?"

"Nothing that stands out in my memory, Mr. Caulfield. We took a tour of the town . . . saw an

141

exhibit of snakes . . . took about a reel of home movies."

Caulfield brightened. "Do you have those movies? And could I see 'em?"

"They're downstairs in the rumpus room. Bru filed all our films in a tin box." She was frowning. "How does this tie in with—"

"Right now, I have to tell you, I may be clutching at the proverbial straws," admitted Caulfield, getting up. "But you've humored me this far. Don't stop now."

Kay stood. "All right, come on down to the rumpus room."

A stagecoach came rattling into the dusty street of Flat Rock. The driver was sprawled on the driving seat, an arrow planted in his back. Townspeople came hurrying up to him.

"They were making a real movie there that day," Kay explained in the darkness, as the color film wound its way through the projector.

A shot of young Charlie, also in cowboy gear, watching open-mouthed.

A black-shirted outlaw clutched his chest and went toppling off the general store roof. The camera didn't quite follow him, but caught up with him as

142

he landed in a foam pad and was helped out of it by a crew member.

"Bru got a big kick out of watching them make this silly cowboy film," Kay said, as the home movie flickered out and ended. "He never knew it took so much time just to do one simple scene. He told me he'd never have the patience for anything like that."

She crossed the darkened room and turned on the lights. "Charlie loved it, too, even though he was coming down with the flu. He was very critical of TV for a while after that. The most impressive stunts didn't impress him. He said no matter how real something looked, it was probably a fake."

"Holy Christ." Caulfield was on his feet, almost hopping.

"I take it you got something out of our little film?"

"He talked about going to a place he really hadn't been," Caulfield said, mostly to himself. "Where he really had been was a place where they could make fake things look real. Holy Christ."

"You said that before," put in Kay. "What exactly are you getting at?"

Impulsively, Caulfield bobbed up to her and kissed her on the forehead. "You'll be the first to know," he said. "Now I really have to get back to work. Thanks."

Before Kay could reply, the newsman was bounding up the rumpus room steps and out the front door.

CHAPTER 27

THE DAY was waning, the light dropping out of the sky.

Willis was making his way along a ridge—weaving, staggering, wobbling. He fell to one knee, got up, and tottered on.

"Talk to me," he urged himself aloud, his wheezing voice coming out through dry, blistered lips. "Tell me . . . jokes . . . keep me company . . ."

The sun seemed to be falling down through the darkening sky.

"Have you heard the one about . . . guy takes trip to Europe?"

Willis fell, hard, on both knees this time. Clutching at rocks, he pulled himself upright.

"Where was I . . . takes a trip to Europe . . . see, it's his first vacation . . . in a long time and . . ."

The ground all around was fading, turning gray.

"So . . . anyway . . . it's his first vacation in . . . long time . . . he sees the . . ."

He lost his footing, went sliding down the rocky side of the ridge. He tried to halt his slide, grabbing out with his hands. That only made them bleed more. At last he came to a stop against a clump of prickly shrubs.

Flat-out, facedown, he stayed there. Breathing in and out, slowly and carefully, through his open mouth.

"So this guy . . . he has a real good time . . . and . . . after a while he decides to call home . . ."

With a little luck, he figured, he could make his way down to what looked like a gully some ten feet below. Climbing back up to the ridge wasn't going to be possible. He'd rest here a moment first, though.

The day was completely done. Darkness was filling the gully.

"Okay, so he gets his . . . his brother on the phone . . . asks him, 'How's everything at home?' Brother says, 'Your cat died.' "

Willis, crawling on hands and knees, worked his way around the brush. He struggled to his feet, tripped, and went rolling and tumbling the rest of the way down the hillside.

145

He hit bottom on his back, sprawled out. He waited for a minute, then decided he was still conscious. Stay like this for a bit, rest before going on.

"Stop me if you've heard this . . . one. . . . Guy tells his brother, 'You shouldn't tell me bad news so . . . bluntly . . . I'm all the way over here . . . in Europe, for Christ sake.' His brother . . . asks him, 'What the hell should I say then?' "

He saw lights in the newly black sky. Red and green lights.

" 'You should break it to me . . . gently . . . you know . . . like . . . you say something like, The cat crawled out on the roof . . . chasing a squirrel . . . and got stuck . . . so we had to call the fire department. . . . It took them an hour . . .' "

The lights were getting bigger, brighter. And there was noise now.

" 'The fireman who climbed up the ladder . . . he got hold of the cat . . . except on the way down he . . . slipped . . . slipped and fell . . . and the cat dropped to the ground . . .' "

A new kind of light. Bright yellow, a beam of it sweeping the ridge. Willis sat up, with considerable effort, and shielded his eyes with one bloody hand.

" 'We took your cat to the vet . . . but they couldn't save it.' See? That's how . . . you ought to break bad news to me."

The yellow light had caught him, was shining on him from directly above.

"Then the guy asks . . . asks his brother, 'So how's mom?' And his brother . . . says, 'She's on the roof.' Get that? He says . . ."

The helicopter was about thirty feet above him now, the beam of light watching him.

"I guess," said Willis, trying to stand, "the scavenger hunt is over."

Kelloway crossed his office to look again at the air conditioner. It was set on low. Room felt awfully chilly for a setting like that. He turned the thing entirely off, and went back to his desk.

The phone rang.

"Yes?"

"Found number two, Dr. Kelloway."

He stiffened. "Who? Was it—"

"Willis. It's Willis."

"And he was alone?"

"Yes, all by himself. Heading south, sir."

"Okay, that means Brubaker went west. Put everybody in that direction," ordered Kelloway. "Two out of three isn't good enough."

"We don't anticipate any trouble, sir."

Kelloway hung up. "No trouble," he said softly.

CHAPTER 28

CAULFIELD spread open the gas station map on his desk next to the ordinance maps. With his Pentel he circled Houston. "Now if Elliot's guess was reasonably accurate—"

The phone on his desk rang.

Caulfield kept studying his maps, and the phone kept ringing.

Finally he answered it. "What?"

"Step into my office," suggested a raspy voice.

"Now?" asked Caulfield, eyes still on his assortment of maps.

"Now would be a dandy time."

"Okay, okay." He pronged the phone, gave a final glance at the maps, and worked his way across the newsroom to knock on a door marked Assignment Editor.

"In, come in."

Caulfield went in to Walter Loughlin's office. "I'm here in answer to your urgent summons, Walter, but I really ought—"

"Stand there, let me gaze upon you." Loughlin was a pudgy man in his early fifties. Until recently he'd smoked several cigars a day, and his lips still had a slight quirk at one side. "I'd almost forgotten what you look like, Robert."

"Walter, can we spare the ironic asides?" Caulfield approached the gray metal desk. "Look, I'm into something and—"

"Your ass is going to be into a sling," his boss assured him.

"You're from the movie-nurtured generation, Walter." He slouched down into a chair. "That's why you try to be Pat O'Brien or Spencer Tracy. Tough city editor on big-town metropolitan sheet."

"Let's change the subject," said Loughlin. "Where the hell have you been?"

Caulfield held up his hands and spread them wide apart. "Look, let's be calm and mature about this, okay? I'd better talk to you, because I think I'm onto something. Really."

"What? Another of your famed scoops?"

"Something is wrong, Walter, something big," said Caulfield. "Big enough so they're trying to kill me."

Loughlin blinked. "Who's trying to kill you? Is it some group I can make a contribution to?"

"Walter, I am not trying to con you, for Christ sake. I mean, they are trying to knock me off."

"Who?"

"I don't think you'd believe me."

"Give it a try."

"Well, a friend of mine, young guy who works with NASA, he gave me a sort of a tip," explained Caulfield. "Then he disappeared."

"Disappeared? In a puff of smoke?"

"He disappeared, Walter, as though he'd never existed. There's a girl living in his apartment now, the furniture is all different, and she says she's been living there for years. She's even got magazines, months old, with her address on them."

"So does my dentist. So?"

"I checked with the building rental office," said Caulfield. "They have receipts from this broad for more than a year. Not only that, they say Elliot Whitter never lived in any of their apartments. Even if I'd made a mistake on the apartment number, which I didn't, they claim they never heard of him. And on top of that, NASA says my friend never worked for them. They maintain nobody there has ever heard of him. Even the phone company tells me he's never had a phone."

"I'd say your friend is a nonperson for sure."

Caulfield gestured at the boss' desk. "Look him up in the phone directory." He leaned back and waited.

Scowling, Loughlin did that. "Here he is, right here. Elliot Whitter, 1284 Claridge."

"Sure, because you can whisk Elliot away, and you can print up some magazine address labels, and you can bribe a few people to change their records," said Caulfield, grinning. "But you can't print a few million fake Houston phone books and have your spies switch them."

Loughlin settled back in his chair. "Who has him?"

"I don't know. Maybe the same people who are trying to knock me off."

"You're trying to tell me that when you decided to go swimming in your car, that wasn't an accident?"

"Okay, I know the cops said there wasn't anything wrong with the car," said Caulfield. "But I guarantee you that the gas pedal and the brakes, and Lord knows what else, had been tampered with."

"Hard to prove at this date."

"And then somebody tried to shoot me."

"When?"

"Yesterday."

"Fortunately, I have an alibi."

"I'm not scamming you, Walter."

"You could be a damn good newsman, Caulfield," said his boss. "If you weren't so fascinated by booze and the ladies. Even as it is, you're not bad. But most of the time you just don't pay your dues. Woodward and Bernstein, the superstars of our field, they work at it. You goof off as much as you dig. For instance, like the time you told me you knew where Patty Hearst was."

"I knew where she'd *been*, not where she was. If you'd backed me up, Walter, we could have started from there and followed the trail to—"

"All right, maybe." He drummed his plump fingertips on the desk top. "A short while ago a trainload of propane gas derailed near Galveston. There's a possibility the town might blow up. I've been sincerely hoping you could join the film crew, which is, even as we speak, waiting at the airport for you."

"Walter, I can't go to Galveston."

"I figured you'd say that."

"When a reporter tells his editor he's working on a big story, the editor is supposed to tell him he's got forty-eight hours to bring back the yarn, or he's finished."

Loughlin drummed his fingers a few more times. "I saw that movie, too. And what the editor gave him was twenty-four hours. Which is what I'm giving you."

Caulfield popped to his feet. "Thanks, chief."

"One more thing," called Loughlin as Caulfield headed for the door. "I still don't much like you. So if you fuck this up, I really will can you. Understand?"

"It's crystal clear," answered Caulfield, and left.

CHAPTER 29

"I HAD one clean cup left." Coffee pot in his right hand, Caulfield was circling the small kitchen of his apartment in his stocking feet.

He studied the contents of the sink again, and poked at the scatter of unwashed dishes and cups. The drainboard was empty, as was the cupboard shelf where he kept meaning to store his clean dishware.

Settling for a cup that looked relatively clean, and swishing it out under the tap, he poured himself a cup of coffee. He set the pot on the stove and returned to his small living room.

He'd brought his collection of maps home, and spread them out on his unmade sofa bed. Using Houston as the center dot, he'd drawn a circle with a radius of 300 miles on a couple of the more detailed maps.

Balancing the cup on his knee, Caulfield sat on the edge of the bed and commenced studying the maps.

It was a warm night and some sort of insects were making tiny chirping sounds outside his window.

Caulfield went over the circle with his fingertip. "Got to be somewhere around here," he murmured, "because Elliot's good with numbers and—"

Blam!

The front door to his apartment came smashing open. Three enormous men leaped in, all armed with guns.

The largest swung and pointed his .38 revolver at Caulfield. "Freeze," he ordered.

"I'm frozen," said Caulfield, eying the three dark-suited men. "And who might—"

"Are you Robert A. Caulfield?"

Caulfield swallowed. "Yeah," he said. "Who the hell are you?"

"Federal agents. We have a warrant to search your apartment."

"I'm going to stand up now," said Caulfield,

gingerly rising. "Now, can I see some kind of proof you fellas are who you claim!"

The spokesman kept his gun leveled at Caulfield's chest. "Show him."

Another of the big men produced an I.D. and a very official looking warrant.

"What exactly are you hunting—"

"Stand aside, Mr. Caulfield," demanded the agent who talked.

The other two went to work on his apartment. They grabbed the maps off the bed, then the sheets. One of them took the cushions off the chairs. The other looked behind the pictures.

"If you find my clean cup I'd—"

"Anything you say can be used against you," said the agent who stood with the .38 aimed at Caulfield's chest. "Best idea is to keep your mouth shut."

"Do I get in trouble if I ask you what you're looking for?"

One of the other agents called from the bathroom, "Come in here, look at this."

"Would you come with me, Mr. Caulfield?"

Caulfield followed him into the small bathroom. "Would you believe this is the most people I've ever had in my john?"

The agent who was already in there pointed to the top shelf in the medicine cabinet, and a small plastic bag filled with white powder. "We just spotted this," he said. He lifted the bag off the shelf, opened it, and took a sniff. After rubbing a pinch of the white substance between his fingers, he handed the bag to the other agent.

This man went through the same sniffing and feeling routine. "Mr. Caulfield, I'm afraid you're under arrest for possession of cocaine."

"I don't believe this," said Caulfield. "You guys put it there. I mean, I've never had dope in here in my life. I am strictly a booze man. What the hell is this? You guys come in here and plant—"

"You have a right to remain silent. You have the right to an attorney."

"Listen, you know damn well that wasn't there when you came in here. You . . ." Watching their faces, he let that sentence die. "Is this what happened to Elliot? Did you frame him on some asshole charge and—"

The third man came into the bathroom, twisted one of Caulfield's arms behind his back, and started to apply handcuffs.

"Hey, that hurts. You don't have to cuff me, I'm not a—"

"Mr. Caulfield, the charges against you already are very serious," advised the man with the gun. "Don't add to them by resisting arrest."

"Saying ouch is resisting arrest? Jesus!" He didn't say anything more. He kept silent while they led him away.

CHAPTER **30**

CAULFIELD came down the steps of the police station and looked up and down the middle-of-the-night street.

To his left a horn honked, and then a car came rolling toward him.

"A friendly face at last," he said, sliding into the passenger seat. "I appreciate this."

"Well, if your own network won't give you a lift," said a sleepy-eyed Judy Drinkwater, "somebody has to."

"Loughlin got me bailed out," said Caulfield, as the girl guided the car away from the curb. "But that's as far as it went. He maintains that since I'm no longer an NBC employee, he can't give me free rides."

"They fired you?"

"Turns out there's something in the NBC code of ethics against employing junkies."

"You're not a junkie."

"Thanks."

"A boozer and a lecher and a chauvinist, yes. But otherwise you're as clean-cut as Jack Armstrong."

Caulfield reached over and put his hand on hers briefly. "I wasn't even sure when I phoned you, and woke you up, if you'd come gather me up, Judy."

"Told you the sincere approach works with me," she said. "You tell me about the lonely plight of the dedicated newsperson, or the dilemma of the individual in a mass society, and it doesn't work. But call me and tell me you're in a jam, out on bail, and minus a job, and I rush right over."

"You're true blue," said Caulfield. "I think I have a tension headache." He rubbed at the back of his neck. "Did you ever have three federal agents pointing guns at you?"

"Never more than two."

"Well, it's a swell way to have the puckey scared out of you." He slouched into the seat, watching the night roll by outside. "Did you find out what I asked you to?"

"For a romantic, you come up with some great

things to ask in the middle of the night, Bob. Judy, go find out all the military installations in a 300-mile radius of Houston."

"Now that we're all equal, guys don't say romantic stuff to ladies anymore. Did you find out?"

"One. White Bluff. It's a SAC base. My father used to be stationed there."

Caulfield slowly shook his head. "White Bluff. Nope. Too big."

"Too big for what?"

"Too big for what I want."

"What do you want?"

"Thinking of enlisting."

"They'll never take you."

"That's why I'm thinking of enlisting."

"Always evasive, Bob." She pulled up in front of an apartment complex. "Is all this part of the same mess? The bases and your getting busted and all?"

"Afraid so."

The girl sighed. "Never thought I'd be helping you on a story."

"The spirit of détente is in the air everywhere." He glanced out the window. "This is your place."

"I was going to invite you to spend the night, or what's left of it."

"Oh, so? I must remember to get busted more often." He frowned. "You sure there's no others besides White Bluff?"

"No, except for an abandoned base they used for training back in World War II. Jackson. Nothing there now," she said, studying his face. "I have the impression you aren't overly anxious to dally."

"I am, really," he assured her. "I love you and all that. Where the hell is Jackson?"

"About 300 miles directly east."

Caulfield put his hand on her shoulder. "How much money do you have on you?"

"Something under a hundred bucks," she replied. "I was going to leave it on the bureau in the morning, but if you prefer to be paid in advan—"

"Loan me the hundred, Judy," he said. "And your car."

After a few thoughtful seconds, she reached into her purse. "You remind me of a mugger I ran into once. Here."

"You're a brick," he said. He laughed. "Always wanted to say that to somebody."

"Can we drop the clever badinage for a minute, Bob? I mean, I'd hate to see you . . . well, get hurt."

"They've tried to drown me, shoot me, and railroad me into prison," he told her. "Failed every time. Face it, I've got a charmed life."

"Up to now." She bent to him and kissed him once on the cheek. "Be careful, whatever the hell it is you're up to. And come back."

"I have to come back," he said. "To finish up

this affair of ours. With such a terrific beginning and middle, it's bound to have a socko ending." He gave her a gentle, propelling pat on the backside. "Get some rest. I'm Jackson-bound."

"Okay." She left the auto. "Good luck."

"The luck of the Caulfields is proverbial," he assured her. He gave her a grin and a lopsided salute, and drove off.

CHAPTER 31

IT went on forever.

It went on forever, and he'd never get out.

No matter where Brubaker looked, with his sand-gritted eyes, he saw red desert. Sand and rock. And the sun, dominating the hazy sky and burning every drop of moisture out of him. Turning him into dust. Dust that a burning wind would scatter away to nothing.

"Come on," he urged himself in the strange croaking voice which was now his. "You're going goofy. Shape up."

Nothing about him was the same. The desert had changed him. His clothes were shredded, his flesh cracked and blistered and incredibly dry. There were scratches scribbled all over him. He couldn't see very well, couldn't even walk without wobbling and stumbling.

The desert refused to end, and he was going to die here.

"Shape up," he croaked to himself again. "You're going to live, goddamn it! Live and fix all these bastards."

Something loomed on the right. A huge mound of red rock. Enough rock to make shade.

Brubaker laughed. Even such a small boon as a little shade, a little protection from the burning sun, could cheer him tremendously. He tried to run to it, but he fell.

And while he lay sprawled in the sand, he heard the sound.

He knew it as well as the running prisoner knows the baying of the dogs. A copter.

"They never give up, those sons of bitches. Never give up."

He crawled, crawled in a desperate, hurrying way. Struggling, fighting to reach the slim sanctuary of the rocks.

When you listen for something so intensely, listen for it even when you're trying to snatch a little sleep, you sometimes think you hear it when it isn't there.

This wasn't a hallucination, though. There was a chopper come hunting him again.

164

He made it to the rocks, dragged himself into a strip of shade. He caught his breath, though that caused his throat and lungs to blaze with pain.

"Not going to catch me," he vowed.

He was going to make it, going to survive. And pay them back. Every damn one of them. Kelloway and all those crew-cut bastards in the "sincere" suits.

After a while, in a setup like this, everything drops away. Life becomes very simple. You stay alive, and you wait for the time when you get your revenge.

He was going to have his revenge. They weren't going to rob him of that.

The sound grew, those blades chopping at the air.

"They didn't see me," he said, nearly certain of that. "But they will."

He raised his head, glanced around. A few feet away was a darker spot in the shadows. Some kind of cave formed between the rocks. If he could get in there, then he'd be safe.

It seemed to take a hell of a time, crawling through the shade to that hole. All the while the copter came closer and closer.

Finally, he was inside. There was hardly enough room for him. By tucking in his legs, he fit.

They were almost directly overhead.

It took Brubaker almost half a minute to become aware of the other sound—a dry rattling sound, coming from the snake that was about two feet from his head.

The barbed wire fence was in sad shape, and the warning sign was so faded by time that it no longer held any threat. *Jackson Army Air Force Base. Closed December 12, 1947. Authorized Personnel Only!*

Caulfield parked his borrowed car off the desert road and hopped out. About a quarter of a mile away was an old hangar. "This could be the place."

He lifted the old barbed wire with caution and crawled under it. He walked across a dry field to the hangar, wary.

Nothing happened, nobody challenged him.

There was a formidable lock on the hangar doors. An old lock, but one that would require a struggle to pick. Slowly, Caulfield circled the building. No windows. The only other door was also locked.

Then he noticed the ventilation opening. The louvered cover didn't look too sturdy. Kneeling, he got it off and set it aside. He peered into the opening. All he saw was the inside of the vent. It looked large enough for a reasonably slim newsman to get through, however.

He decided to try.

Caulfield emerged, considerably dusty, in a totally empty hangar. Every step he took around the place echoed.

"This doesn't bode too well for my theory," he said, kicking at the dusty floor. "Doesn't seem like anybody's been here since the fabulous Forties."

A small amount of sunlight came in through the vent. It turned the dust a golden color.

Caulfield explored the hangar.

It was possible this was the exact spot he was searching for. They could have changed it, made it look exactly as it had.

Possible didn't make any headlines. Facts did. Truths you could prove.

For just an instant something flashed yellow over against the wall. Probably only a mote of dust. He went over to check.

A wedding ring, lying close to the hangar wall, and nearly covered with dust. He blew the dust off, sneezed, and squinted at the inscription, which ran around the ring's inside.

"Holy moley!" he exclaimed, laughing.

Engraved on the ring were the words *Bru from Kay 6/13/64.*

Caulfield closed his fingers around the ring. "Gotcha," he said.

CHAPTER 32

THE SNAKE struck, scaly head knifing toward Brubaker's hand.

He jerked his hand away, the snake missed his fingers by less than an inch.

Outside, the chuffing of the helicopter was incredibly loud.

If he backed out, they'd have a nice, clear view of his backside.

The rattling of the snake's tail seemed almost as loud as the puffing of the hovering chopper.

Very slowly and carefully, Brubaker inched his hand away from the snake.

The snake struck again. Missed again, because Brubaker had tucked himself suddenly to the left.

He moved his feet to do that, causing a trickle of sand and gravel to go spewing out of the cave.

They might have seen that.

Brubaker waited.

The snake recoiled, head ticking from side to side.

"Fainter," he said.

Yeah, the sound of the watching copter was a bit fainter.

And now even more faint. They were going away.

Brubaker still didn't move. He waited, counting off seconds inside his head. A minute dragged by. Another.

Then he began to ease back.

Something dug into his chest. A rock. He closed his hand on it. Easing back some, he extended his left hand toward the rattler.

The snake watched the approaching hand, then snapped its head toward it.

But the hand wasn't there. Brubaker brought the rock down with his other hand, hard. He could feel the head of the snake going to pieces beneath the rock. Blood squirted.

He lifted the bloody rock away, watched the quivering body of the rattler.

"Jesus," he said, knowing what he had to do next.

He picked up the dead snake, got himself out of the tiny cave, and sat with his back against the red rocks. From inside the tatters of his jump suit, he took his half of the mirror.

"Wish Willis was here. He could make a joke about this."

Using the mirror for a knife, he skinned the rattler and hacked its flesh into strips.

Staying alive and free was all that counted.

With no hesitation, he picked up a strip of snake meat and put it in his mouth. Methodically he chewed and swallowed.

It squatted in the dry field, lopsided and weather-beaten—part barn, part hangar; tin-roofed, with a hand-painted sign on its side announcing *A & A Cropdusting Service*.

Trailing dust and exhaust fumes, Caulfield drove along the drive which led to this forlorn building. Parked in front of the building was an ancient biplane, which might still fly. It also had *A&A* painted on its side.

After parking, Caulfield approached the plane.

He was afraid that if he trod too heavily, it might collapse in a heap of wood and wire.

"Yeah?"

A hairless man in an orange jump suit had emerged from the barn-hangar, lugging a jug of chemicals. "You in charge here?" Caulfield inquired.

The man was about fifty, as weather-beaten as his building. He set the jug at his feet and fished a faded Houston Astros baseball cap out of a lumpy pocket. "You look to me like a big city smart ass."

"I have to admit I am. Now are—"

"See that advertisement on the side of my hangar?"

"I noticed it. Said A & A Cropdusting Service."

"You know who I am?"

"I bet you're one of those A's."

"Which one? Do you know the answer to that, smart ass?"

Caulfield scratched his chin. "The first one."

"Wrong."

"Give me one more guess?"

"You got her."

"You're the second A."

"Wrong again." He clamped the baseball cap on his bald head. "I am both of them A's. How you like that, smart ass? Name is Albain. I got a son, and he used to be the other A. He didn't think much of flying, and went off to be a lawyer. So I decided

I got a schmuck for a son, and I took his A away from him, thereby making myself both. So if you're looking for the man in charge, you are gazing directly on both of 'em."

"Pleased to meet you. My name is Caulfield."

"We all got our crosses to bear."

"Mr. Albain, how much do you charge to dust a field?"

"Twenty-five bucks."

"Well, I'd like to hire your . . . uh . . . plane," said Caulfield, very carefully patting the side of the relic.

"That'll be one hundred bucks."

"Hey, you said the fee was twenty-five."

"Nope, I said it was twenty-five smackers to dust a field. But you haven't got no field, because you obviously ain't no farmer. Which also means you ain't poor, smart ass."

"Okay, a hundred."

"It'll be a hundred twenty-five."

"Huh?"

"You said okay to a hundred too quick. Meaning you can go higher."

Caulfield dug into his pocket and got his wallet. He removed all his cash. "I don't suppose you're on Visa? Let's see . . . I've got exactly one hundred and twenty-six bucks here, Mr. Albain. Suppose we settle for a fee of a hundred, so as I'll—"

"No dough, no go."

"Hundred and twenty?"

"One twenty-five was the agreed-on price, smart ass."

"Well, I suppose I can always wire home for more." He gave Albain all but his last dollar. "If I had a home."

"Hop aboard." The pilot indicated the rear of the two open seats. "And tell me where you want to go."

"I'm not sure," he said, climbing up into the cockpit. "We're going looking for someone who's lost."

"It's your money," said Albain, climbing into the front seat. "We can waste it any way you want, smart ass."

CHAPTER 33

AT FIRST he didn't believe it.

Brubaker stopped still, staring. The road didn't go away.

Not much of a road, but the damn thing was real. A paved road, built by people, cutting across the desert.

And down that road, not more than a quarter mile away, stood a gas station. A run-down, once-white, old wreck of a gas station, and the first building he'd seen since he left the downed jet such a long time ago.

With considerable effort, he could make his body

run—a lopsided imitation of running, but it got him off the sand and onto that road, taking him, painful minutes later, to the gas station.

"Hey!" he shouted in his croak of a voice. "Hey!"

Only a hot dry silence.

The lone gas pump was dented and rusty. Brubaker caught hold of it, to keep himself from falling over. "Hey, you got a customer out here!"

Spider webs all over the dirty windows and the weathered wooden door of the clapboard station building.

"Jesus, it's abandoned."

Brubaker forced himself to walk to the door. He got hold of the knob, turned it. The door was locked.

He stayed, leaning against the door, for a long time. Then he backed off and charged at it, backed and charged again. The old door gave way as its rusty hinges screeched. The whole door fell into the station office, with Brubaker on top of it.

"Come on, come on," he urged himself. "Dumb to quit now."

He got up, caught hold of a counter, and surveyed the room. There were some cans of oil in a rack against the wall, one tire leaning in a corner. And on the wall a telephone.

"Pay telephone. And it was probably disconnected years ago."

Maybe not. Maybe the owner of this station had

only recently left. Maybe he was even planning to come back.

Brubaker spotted the cash register. Sitting at the far end of the counter. He worked his way over to it, pushed at its various buttons with his battered fingers.

"Calm," he said. "Push the damn *No Charge* tab."

He did. Nothing happened. The money drawer stayed tightly shut.

"Got to be some tools around this dump. Find them and—"

Crash!

In turning away, his elbow had slammed into the cash register, sent it sailing off the counter to the plank floor. With a thumping, jingling sound, the drawer popped open.

Two dirty and crumpled dollar bills fell out.

Brubaker dropped to his knees. "Look, I can't get change for these around here, damn it."

He poked a finger into the compartments. Hit something. Felt like a dime. It was.

Very carefully he extracted the coin, placed it in the center of his blistered palm and rose. He went tottering to the wall phone.

Holding his breath, he dropped the coin into the slot. He had the receiver pressed to his ear. "Come on, please. Give me a dial tone."

Nothing happened. Ten seconds went by. Then the phone began to hum at him.

Brubaker made a rumbling sound that was supposed to be a laugh, and dialed 0.

"May I help you?" said a female voice.

"Yeah, you may," said Brubaker.

"I'm sorry, sir, I can't hear you very well. Can you speak up?"

He did the best shouting he was capable of. "I want to make a collect call to Houston, Texas," he said.

Caulfield was dividing his time between ignoring the stomach-churning quality of the flight and staring down at the glaring desert below, for some trace of the astronauts he expected to find.

"Imagine giving this up to be a lawyer!" Albain shouted back at him, as the old biplane lurched.

"Not smart," he replied through cupped hands.

They were flying a few hundred feet over the desert, and had been in the air for nearly an hour. Thus far they'd spotted only a dead coyote. Caulfield wasn't certain what he was looking for. He was sure that at least Brubaker had been at the hangar until recently. But where he and the other two astronauts were at the moment, Caulfield had no clear idea. They'd been in this area, so maybe they still were. Or some sign of them.

"What the hell's your friend doing out here, anyhow?" inquired the baldheaded pilot, as he banked the craft.

"Lost."

"He rob a bank or something? Hijack an airliner?"

"Nope."

"I get a third!"

"Huh?"

"We find him, I get a third of the loot."

The venerable biplane lurched again.

Caulfield clutched at his stomach, nodding. "Sure, sure."

CHAPTER 34

IT HAD rung twenty times. He let it ring ten more before he hung up.

"All right, Kay's not home. So I'll try somebody else, Pete's wife or Jack's."

His dime didn't come back.

Brubaker thrust his forefinger into the coin return slot. Empty.

He slammed the side of the wall phone with the side of his fist.

No dime.

He lifted the receiver, listened. He'd lost the dial tone. He snapped the holder up and down, then hung the phone up.

No dime.

Brubaker went back to the fallen cash register, knelt beside it.

"If I can find one more dime, a couple nickels, anything . . ."

Then he heard the helicopters—a pair of them —huffing and puffing, closer and closer.

Brubaker crawled across the floor to one of the dirt-smeared front windows of the station.

The copters were hovering over the roadway, only a few yards above it.

Obviously, they were going to land. They probably had no idea he was here, but they were going to check out this ramshackle old building anyway.

Thorough, that's what they were. Didn't pass up anything.

The helicopters set down on the desert, which framed the narrow road.

Brubaker stopped watching and glanced around the room.

There wasn't anywhere he could hide. Nothing he could use as a weapon.

Very carefully, he peered again through the front window. Two men were disembarking from one of the helicopters. Both carried pistols.

"Wonder what Kelloway's orders are? Could be to get me back any way they can, dead or alive."

The two men were coming straight for the station.

180

Caulfield made a face and scratched at his nose. The searching, outside of inverting his stomach, was having no results. "Maybe," he called out to his hairless pilot, "we should try another direction."

"Over there!"

"What?"

"Over there, smart ass!" Albain jerked a finger in the direction of a narrow strip of road.

Two helicopters were sitting on the ground, only a hundred yards or so from a run-down gas station. "Could be something," said Caulfield.

"Been seeing them around, last couple days. Could be they're looking for your friend, too."

"Okay. Can you case that setup?"

"Ain't I proved my ability to fly by now?"

Albain guided his ancient crop-dusting plane down toward the gas station.

Eyes narrowed, Caulfield watched the roadway. "Two guys."

"Two guys with guns!"

"Somebody must be in that building, and they're going after him," decided Caulfield. "We got to land."

"Remember those guns."

"You're getting a third of the loot."

"Better make that half."

"Okay, you got it."

He stopped breathing. Brubaker stood pressed to the wall inside the gas station, flat beside the door.

Footsteps slowly came nearer.

"Somebody did a job on this door," said a voice outside.

Brubaker very quietly let out a breath, waiting.

"Go easy," advised a second voice. "I'll back you up."

What was left of the door came slamming inward, away from Brubaker.

A gun came floating into the room, held by a gloved hand.

When half of the arm, clad in green jump suit cloth, was in, Brubaker dealt a savage chop to the arm.

The man yelled, his gun smacked the wooden floor.

Brubaker jumped, keeping the man between himself and the second green-suited man.

He brought up his knee and caught the man in the groin. Ducking, he hit him hard with his shoulder.

The man went flying out of the room and smack into his partner.

182

Brubaker, diving and scooping up the fallen gun, went dashing across the room. He tensed and went diving through the back window.

"This might be something," remarked Albain, as glass came exploding out into the bright desert day. The biplane, prop still turning, had just settled down behind the station.

"Christ, it looks like Brubaker!" Caulfield stood up in his seat, waved his arms. "Brubaker, over here."

"He the one we're looking for?"

"Yeah, yeah, get closer."

Albain taxied toward the stumbling astronaut.

A man in a green jump suit, after brushing away jagged shards of glass with a gloved hand, was climbing out the window Brubaker had gone through. When he hit the ground, he pointed his pistol skyward and fired once.

"This beats dusting crops," said Albain, with a pleased chuckle.

"And it's only just starting." They were very close to Brubaker now. Caulfield leaned far out. "Come on, get aboard!"

Brubaker, his face twisted with pain, was trying to reach the lower wing of the biplane.

"Company," said Albain.

One of the helicopters had come bobbing over the gas station.

Brubaker got hold of a strut and pulled himself onto the wing.

"Take her up!" urged Caulfield. "Jesus, get us in the air and out of here!"

"Here we go, everybody hang on."

The old plane swung around and went bouncing along the dusty ground. The helicopter was getting close, and now the second one rose into view.

The rear wheel of Albain's plane bounced once, twice, and then was free of the ground, as it rose into the sky.

Brubaker hugged the strut as the biplane rose higher and higher. He stared at Caulfield. "I know you," he shouted in a croaking voice.

"Caulfield, NBC," the newsman yelled back. "Please, hold on real well. You're my big story of the year."

"Everybody get set," announced Albain. "We're going to do a little evasive flying." He yanked the stick, and the biplane commenced climbing.

Both copters had been gaining on them.

Albain's plane went roaring upward, banked, and then executed a series of loops and dives which considerably confused the opposition.

Brubaker didn't know how much longer he could keep his grip on the wing strut. This was like something out of an old air carnival, and he really wasn't in shape for it.

Albain had gained some distance on the helicopters. Now he was diving toward the desert. About three miles dead ahead loomed a high ridge of orange and gold rock. He seemed to be directing his old plane straight for it.

"Lawyers!" he shouted. "What do they know? This is the only way to live!"

"Speaking of living," shouted Caulfield, using his hands for a megaphone, "we'd like to continue with it."

"No fear, smart ass."

One of the copters was cutting the distance, chuffing up on them. And the second wasn't far behind.

"Going to be a humdinger!" Albain was roaring right for the rocky ridge. "Hold your noses!"

All at once there was a blinding cloud of white pouring out of the tail of the plane. Albain had released his crop dusting chemicals, and very swiftly the stuff was swirling all around.

Albain again tugged on the stick, and the biplane climbed. Climbed enough to clear the ridge.

The copters were not so lucky. They collided in the fog of chemical spray and went plummeting downward.

On the other side of the ridge, Albain leveled out

185

and bobbed his head up and down with satisfaction. "Now that's flying!"

"It is, it is," agreed Caulfield, as he helped Brubaker climb into the cockpit.

CHAPTER 35

THE PRESIDENT of the United States arrived at the cemetery.

Everyone stood up.

There were several hundred spectators on the rolling green lawns and two dozen or more people on the temporary stage that had been set up. In the front row were Kay Brubaker, Janet Willis, and Elizabeth Walker, as well as Dr. Kelloway, Congressman Peaker, and the Vice President.

The President reached the platform exactly as the military band finished playing "Hail to the Chief." He walked directly to the lectern.

Everyone sat down.

"Ladies and gentlemen, Mrs. Brubaker, Mrs. Willis, Mrs. Walker, my fellow Americans," he began. "I come here today to talk of unfinished hopes and of unfulfilled dreams. Charles Brubaker, Peter Willis, and John Walker left this earth because of their dream a little more than two months ago. They were never able to return to us. . . ."

As the President spoke, Kelloway lowered his head and eyed his intertwined fingers.

". . . a time when cynicism was a national epidemic, they gave us something to take pride. . . ."

Kay was not going to cry. She had made up her mind about that. Beside her, Janet Willis had brought her handkerchief up to touch her face. Not looking at her, Kay put a hand on her arm.

". . . dream that should not be allowed to die. A nation is built on the spirit of its people. The test of greatness of any nation is how that nation pulls together in time of crisis . . ."

At the far edge of the crowd, a slight commotion was beginning. A few people stood up, there was a murmuring.

". . . these three men brought us together. We knew there were no goals we couldn't reach, so long as we reach for them together. . . ."

The President paused for a few seconds. The commotion was spreading. Someone was moving through the crowd, toward the podium, and the Secret Service men were moving toward him.

"There is no adequate way we can ever express our gratitude toward these men themselves," continued the President. "However, we can serve their memory. We can pay homage to them in a way which is more than mere oratory. We can see to it that what they gave their lives for, was not an abandoned dream. Therefore, I am proud to announce that today I have asked the leaders of both Houses of Congress to increase the appropriations for the space . . ."

Kelloway recognized him first, and gasped a startled breath. Then Kay saw him. She stood up, her hands clapping together once. She laughed aloud, crying at the same time.

Brubaker was approaching the podium. The Secret Service men stood aside for him. He still wore the tattered jump suit he'd worn in his escape across the desert.

But he walked very straight, shoulders back. And he was smiling.

BESTSELLERS

☐	BEGGAR ON HORSEBACK–Thorpe	23091-0	1.50
☐	THE TURQUOISE–Seton	23088-0	1.95
☐	STRANGER AT WILDINGS–—Brent	23085-6	1.95
	(Pub. in England as Kirkby's Changeling)		
☐	MAKING ENDS MEET–Howar	23084-8	1.95
☐	THE LYNMARA LEGACY–Gaskin	23060-0	1.95
☐	THE TIME OF THE DRAGON–Eden	23059-7	1.95
☐	THE GOLDEN RENDEZVOUS–MacLean	23055-0	1.75
☐	TESTAMENT–Morrell	23033-3	1.95
☐	CAN YOU WAIT TIL FRIDAY?–	23022-8	1.75
	Olson, M.D.		
☐	HARRY'S GAME–Seymour	23019-8	1.95
☐	TRADING UP–Lea	23014-7	1.95
☐	CAPTAINS AND THE KINGS–Caldwell	23069-4	2.25
☐	"I AIN'T WELL–BUT I SURE AM	23007-4	1.75
	BETTER"–Lair		
☐	THE GOLDEN PANTHER–Thorpe	23006-6	1.50
☐	IN THE BEGINNING–Potok	22980-7	1.95
☐	DRUM–Onstott	22920-3	1.95
☐	LORD OF THE FAR ISLAND–Holt	22874-6	1.95
☐	DEVIL WATER–Seton	22888-6	1.95
☐	CSARDAS–Pearson	22885-1	1.95
☐	CIRCUS–MacLean	22875-4	1.95
☐	WINNING THROUGH INTIMIDATION–	23589-0	2.25
	Ringer		
☐	THE POWER OF POSITIVE	23499-1	1.95
	THINKING–Peale		
☐	VOYAGE OF THE DAMNED–	22449-X	1.75
	Thomas & Witts		
☐	THINK AND GROW RICH–Hill	23504-1	1.95
☐	EDEN–Ellis	23543-2	1.95

Buy them at your local bookstores or use this handy coupon for ordering:

FAWCETT BOOKS GROUP, 1 Fawcett Place, P.O. Box 1014, Greenwich, Ct.06830

Please send me the books I have checked above. Orders for less than 5
books must include 60¢ for the first book and 25¢ for each additional book to
cover mailing and handling. Postage is FREE for orders of 5 books or more.
Check or money order only. Please include sales tax.

Name_____   Books $_____
Address_____   Postage _____
                                         Sales Tax _____
City_____State/Zip_____   Total $_____

Please allow 4 to 5 weeks for delivery. This offer expires 12/78.

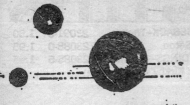

OUTER SPACE

Isaac Asimov

☐	BEFORE THE GOLDEN AGE, Book I	C2913	1.95
☐	BEFORE THE GOLDEN AGE, Book II	Q2452	1.50
☐	BEFORE THE GOLDEN AGE, Book III	Q2525	1.50
☐	THE BEST OF ISAAC ASIMOV	23653-6	1.95
☐	BUY JUPITER AND OTHER STORIES	23062-7	1.50
☐	THE CAVES OF STEEL	Q2858	1.50
☐	THE CURRENTS OF SPACE	23507-6	1.50
☐	EARTH IS ROOM ENOUGH	23383-9	1.75
☐	THE END OF ETERNITY	Q2832	1.50
☐	THE GODS THEMSELVES	X2883	1.75
☐	I, ROBOT	Q2829	1.50
☐	THE MARTIAN WAY	23158-5	1.50
☐	THE NAKED SUN	22648-4	1.50
☐	NIGHTFALL AND OTHER STORIES	23188-7	1.75
☐	NINE TOMORROWS	Q2688	1.50
☐	PEBBLE IN THE SKY	23423-1	1.75
☐	THE STARS, LIKE DUST	Q2780	1.50
☐	WHERE DO WE GO FROM HERE?—Ed.	X2849	1.75

Buy them at your local bookstore or use this handy coupon for ordering:

FAWCETT BOOKS GROUP, 1 Fawcett Place, P.O. Box 1014, Greenwich, Ct.06830

Please send me the books I have checked above. Orders for less than 5 books must include 60¢ for the first book and 25¢ for each additional book to cover mailing and handling. Postage is FREE for orders of 5 books or more. Check or money order only. Please include sales tax.

Name_____

Address_____

City_____/_____State/Zip_____

Books $_____
Postage _____
Sales Tax _____
Total $_____

Please allow 4 to 5 weeks for delivery. This offer expires 12/78

A-16